W9-CTV-739

What readers say about Harlequin Romances

"I feel as if I am in a different world every time I read a Harlequin."
A.T.,* Detroit, Michigan

"Harlequins have been my passport to the world. I have been many places without ever leaving my doorstep."
P.Z., Belvedere, Illinois

"I like Harlequin books because they tell so much about other countries."
N.G., Rouyn, Quebec

"Your books offer a world of knowledge about places and people."
L.J., New Orleans, Louisiana

*Names available on request

OTHER
Harlequin Romances
by SARA SEALE

Many of these titles are available at your local bookseller•
or through the Harlequin Reader Service.

For a free catalogue listing all available Harlequin Romances,
send your name and address to:

HARLEQUIN READER SERVICE,
M.P.O. Box 707, Niagara Falls, N.Y. 14302
Canadian address: Stratford, Ontario, Canada N5A 6W2

or use coupon at back of book.

The Truant Spirit

by

SARA SEALE

Harlequin Books

TORONTO • LONDON • NEW YORK • AMSTERDAM
SYDNEY • HAMBURG • PARIS

Original hardcover edition published in 1966
by Mills & Boon Limited

ISBN 0-373-01347-7

Harlequin edition published November 1969

Second printing February 1970
Third printing June 1975
Fourth printing September 1977
Fifth printing March 1979

for Jane Matthews
with thanks for W.W.

———————————◆———————————

Copyright © 1966 by Sara Seale.
Philippine copyright 1979.   Australian copyright 1979.

All rights reserved. Except for use in any review, the reproduction of utilization of
this work in whole or in part in any form by any electronic, mechanical or other
means, now known or hereafter invented, including xerography, photocopying
and recording, or in any information storage or retrieval system, is forbidden
without the permission of the publisher. All the characters in this book have no
existence outside the imagination of the author and have no relation whatsoever
to anyone bearing the same name or names. They are not even distantly
inspired by any individual known or unknown to the author, and all the incidents
are pure invention.

The Harlequin trademark, consisting of the word HARLEQUIN and the portrayal
of a Harlequin, is registered in the United States Patent Office and in the Canada
Trade Marks Office.

Printed in U.S.A.

CHAPTER ONE

SABINA was asleep when the train pulled into the little Cornish junction where she was to change. The journey had seemed endless, and after the first hundred miles the elation of escape had given place to doubts. Was she not foolish to come so far with so little money? Would Marthe inform the police? What difference would it make in the end that she had seen Penruthan for herself and been for a brief few days independent and answerable to no one?

I am myself and all alone, she thought firmly, as the train began to lull her to the resignation and impersonality of all long journeys. *One is One and all alone and ever more shall be so* . . . It was a disquieting thought, but soothing at the same time. The lines of the old rhyme had been running through her head since the train had started . . . *twelve for the Twelve Apostles* . . . *nine for the Nine Bright Shiners* . . . *seven for the Seven who dwell in Heaven* . . . *six for the Six Proud Walkers* . . . The rhythm fitted to the rhythm of the train, and she thought defiantly again: I am myself for the first time . . . But the reflection of her face in the smoky windows as the train passed through tunnels was not reassuring. She looked lost and small and without distinction, and she knew that apart from Tante Lucille and Marthe she had little existence of her own. Her future was already decided, and she too young and too well disciplined to rebel; yet was not rebellion in this very action? To run away while Marthe was visiting a friend had not, perhaps, been very nice, or to flout Tante's wishes when she was far away in the South of France and could not immediately retaliate, but the Six Proud Walkers, whoever they were, would, she felt sure, have struck out for freedom, however temporary, striding away into the unknown . . .

As Sabina began to drift into sleep while the train rattled through anonymous darkness, pictures formed with depressing assurance of the futility of even temporary escape. She remembered Tante accepting responsibility for her when she had been left an orphan, and the years of

5

being pushed into the background because money was scarce and Tante, volatile and restless, must still contrive her trips abroad and her many small comforts; she remembered Marthe's vigilance and endless scoldings, the cheap hotels, the cheaper day-schools where no friends were made, and finally, Tante's plans, coming at last it would seem to maturity.

Sabina had grown up with the French view of marriage and it no longer seemed strange that she should be promised in some vague fashion to the unknown René Bergerac, probably listening at this very moment to Tante's propositions in his far-away château. The life she had led since the death of her father had made her grow up quickly in some matters and slowly in others. At nineteen she had a sobriety that warred constantly with the questions and doubts of adolescence, but, except upon this one day, sobriety had always won, for was she not, as Tante and Marthe frequently pointed out, beholden to charity which could ill be afforded?

At first she had recoiled with mild alarm from her aunt's proposal, but Tante, worldly and a little impatient as always, had soon ridiculed such unsophisticated objections.

"But you are *bourgeoise, ma petite!*" she exclaimed, regarding her niece with a mixture of scorn and exasperation. "Do you dream of the fairy-tale prince who comes to reward all good little girls? That time has gone, *chérie*. Girls work these days and marry a bank clerk without prospects and keep on working to provide the monthly payments on the furniture, or, if they are wise, and have the opportunity, they make the marriage of convenience and let love look after itself."

"But this M. Bergerac might not be agreeable—besides, he is too old," Sabina said, struggling to grasp her aunt's point of view.

"What has age to do with it?" Tante countered indulgently. "When you are not yet twenty the middle years sound a long way off, but they come quickly enough. A rich Frenchman of that age has sown his wild oats—he is ready to *ranger* himself with a wife who is *convenable* and not too demanding. Is there such hardship in taking

6

the famous name of a man who will cherish you like a daughter—with a few reservations, of course?"

"No no . . . but he hasn't seen me."

"He has seen the photograph on which I spent much good money. It was a triumph, that, *hein*—something to make a man think?"

"But not a bit like me—not a bit like anyone I could ever hope to be." .

"Bien sûr," Tante replied indifferently. "But that is no matter. Money can do much, and the Bergeracs have always married for reasonable considerations. René will not be concerned with a wife who is likely to turn his clients' heads, which has its disadvantage in his business; also, the house will be of first importance."

Of course . . . the house . . . thought Sabina, finding it quite normal, if a little discouraging, that the house should be of primary consideration. She had never understood why René Bergerac's mother should have left Penruthan to her, a distant, unimportant relation whom she had never met, but she had appreciated her aunt's chagrin when it was discovered that the place was entailed and could not be sold in Sabina's lifetime. Sabina had always understood that Penruthan was Tante's trump card. René's father, who had made the Château Berger one of the most famous hotels in Europe, had, so it was said, married his wife to acquire the house as an English branch, and his son, said Tante, would do the same to bring it into the family again.

"Not very flattering," Sabina had said once, "to be taken along with the house like—like the caretaker or—or an old dog that has been pensioned."

Tante had given her automatic, artificial laugh, and tapped Sabina on the cheek.

"What an amusing conceit!" she had said. "But you do not have to set your value so low, *ma petite.* René needs a wife as well as a house. It is best that a *hotelier* should be married—it is both a conventional necessity and a protection. You need not fear for your status at Berger. The French uphold family life more rigorously than the British."

"Then, why," asked Sabina, not following her aunt's

philosophy very clearly, "wouldn't he rather marry a Frenchwoman?"

"You are a little stupid, sometimes," Tante replied impatiently. "It is you who happen to own Penruthan, a place too large and demanding to be of any use to you in your lifetime; besides, René's mother was English—that, no doubt, might influence him in the matter of taking a wife. *Mon dieu*, Sabina! Do you not understand that in this way you can repay me for my care of you? Had I known that Penruthan could not be sold I could not have afforded to make myself responsible for you. I was misled on many accounts, and now that you are in a position to offer me a home free from want and worry, you make the difficulties no French girl would contemplate for a moment."

Sabina became humbly aware of the thorn she must have been in Tante's impatient flesh.

"I could work," she said.

Tante laughed.

"Assuredly you could work," she said. "But that would not greatly help me, *chérie*. I will tell you a little secret. When I was younger I spent much time at the Château Berger. René Bergerac *père* had more than a fondness for me. It was, I fear, perhaps on my account that his wife left him, so you see, since she willed her house away from her husband and her son, it is fitting that we should return it, *hein*?"

Even then, Sabina had felt there was something specious about her aunt's arguments, but the habit of obedience was too strong. What did it matter, after all? As time went on and letters passed between the château and their cheap little London hotels, she came to accept the situation just as long ago she had learned to accept Tante's way of life, and Marthe, that uncompromising Frenchwoman who had remained in Tante's service for years, probably without wages, had seen to it that proper gratitude should not be wanting.

"For look you," she would say. "You will never be *chic* or witty like Madame. It is only *convenable* that you should fall in with her wishes, and, believe me, mam'zelle, you are fortunate that such a chance should come your way. Madame is no longer young and it is right that her

8

future should be assured, for, but for her, what future would you yourself look forward to?"

Sabina supposed that this was only just. If Tante had not taken her when she had been left an orphan, what would have become of her?

"This M. Bergerac," she inquired a little timidly, "he is like the head waiter in our hotels?"

Marthe's black eyes were amused.

"The head waiters in our hotels are *canaille*," she replied. "M. Bergerac, if he is anything like his father, would employ none of them in the humblest capacity. Me, I have known the great *hoteliers*—you do not need to fear, mam'zelle . . . The name of Bergerac is famous among the discerning."

"Have you never seen him, then?"

"Not the present Bergerac. He would, I believe, have never become *hotelier* had it not been for his illness. During his father's lifetime he took little interest in the business."

"His illness? He's not—I mean, he's not—ill—in any way now, is he?"

"*Ça dépend*, but—well, I think he is not robust. It is a life in which one can look after the health, you understand. It was an illness, perhaps, that encouraged fears for the digestion and a dislike of fresh air."

"What was the matter with him?"

"I forget, but you should be thankful, mam'zelle. He will not demand so full a life as some. He will be grateful, no doubt, for polite consideration and little else, and that should be enough for an English bride."

For a moment the woman had looked out from the girl's clear eyes, and Marthe's eyebrows lifted as she was asked gently:

"And what of me, Marthe? Don't I merit a—a full life—with someone of my own age—with a strong stomach?"

"You are too young for such matters," Marthe replied a little brusquely. "And Madame would say you are not the type. Now for her—but the English do not understand temperament. Be thankful that for you the future should be smooth, and if Monsieur is not quite to your taste,

9

then—a rich woman can have her—relaxations—if she is clever."

The forthright Frenchwoman's meaning was plain, and Sabina coloured slightly.

"That wasn't what I meant at all," she said, and Marthe turned away with a shrug.

"No? But then at your age, *petite*, you do not know what you want," she observed. "Be guided by Madame, for to her you owe much. Had she not come forward it might have been an institution for you."

"Yes," said Sabina, "I understand."

She did not altogether believe in the familiar allusion to an institution, but she had understood very early on that Tante's generosity had been mainly prompted by the lure of Penruthan, and the tempting price it would fetch in the market. She shared her aunt's disappointment that the place was entailed, and accepted the fact that, between them, she and Penruthan had cheated Tante of just expectations. . . .

The train carried her relentlessly to her unknown destination, to the house which for so long had stood empty and neglected on the edge of a Cornish moor. She had never seen it, and now with Tante only yesterday gone to France to make the final delicate arrangements, she had experienced this unaccountable urge to visit the little Cornish village alone, and find for herself this unwanted legacy which must play such a part in her future.

She was tired and very conscious that her bid for freedom was foolish. In a few weeks Tante would return with M. Bergerac himself to inspect the house and his future bride; and what object had there been in running away?

The rhythm of the train became more hypnotic . . . *Seven are the Seven who dwell in Heaven . . . six are the Six Proud Walkers . . . five are the Flamboys under the boat . . . four are the Gospel Makers . . .*

*　　　*　　　*

She had slipped into a dream which made no sense long before the train stopped with a jerk which threw her across the seat of the empty carriage. She awoke with a start and wondered for the moment where she was. No passengers left the train, and Sabina, hanging out of the window to see where she was, shivered in the cold night air and wished she had not given way to that unusual impulse for self-expression.

The train was about to leave when she saw the name of the station, Kairy, painted on a seat, and, wrenching at the door in panic as she remembered that here she must change, she fell on to the platform as the train began to move. She felt very much alone as she watched the last carriage disappear round a bend in the line. The station seemed deserted and rain was dripping off the glass roof on to her bare head. She had never travelled without Tante or Marthe, and she looked timidly for someone to direct her as to the next procedure. The platforms were devoid of porters; indeed the whole station seemed bereft of life. Ill-lit and ominously quiet except for the wind which whistled in from the outer darkness, it seemed to Sabina a place from which there could be no departure.

She crossed the bridge to the exit and found the ticket-collector already shutting the gates.

"Thought no one got off her tonight," he remarked crossly. "Ticket, please."

It was only then that Sabina realised that in her hurry she had left both her handbag and her suitcase in the train. She tried to explain, wondering miserably how she would manage for the night with nothing but the clothes in which she stood up, but the man merely kept repeating: "If you'm lost ticket you have to pay again."

"But I can't," said Sabina, almost in tears. "I keep telling you I've left everything in the train—my money as well."

He regarded her sourly.

"You'm proper mazed. Where be to?" he said at last.

She was unfamiliar with west-country phraseology, and looked at him blankly.

"Where be going?" he translated more simply. "The folks'll mebbe pay for 'e."

"I'm not staying here," Sabina said. "I'm going to Truan, and I wanted to know which platform the train goes from."

"Not without ticket you don't," the man replied, "That's

11

cheating railways to travel without ticket. They could put 'e in gaol, m'dear."

"But I've told you—can't you ring up the next station and get them to look?"

"Don't stop afore Bodmin, and that's another hour. Last train to Truan will have gone by then."

They stared at each other with dislike; then the ticket-collector made an effort.

"Where be to in Truan?" he asked. "Mebbe you could telephone 'e."

"I—I'm not expected," faltered Sabina. "I thought perhaps there would be an inn—there are always inns in villages, aren't there—somewhere you can stay, I mean?"

He spat over his shoulder and became very official.

"Now that don't sound right to me—it don't sound right at all," he said, and his eyes beneath the peaked cap seemed suddenly menacing. "It's my belief you'm just diddling the railways and haven't no place to go at all. You'd best come with me and see the constable over to police-station. If you'm not diddling railways, then you'm up to no good no ways. You come along o' me."

It did not occur to Sabina in her panic that at the police-station she might have explained her position more satisfactorily; she only thought they would send her back to London, to Marthe and the loss of her first precious freedom.

"No . . . no . . ." she cried, and before he could stop her she was through the little wicket gate in a flash and swallowed up in the darkness beyond.

She ran down a street between huddled cottages, the rain driving in her face. Presently the houses ended and the road stretched dark and lonely into the unknown country. Her steps slowed to a walk and she went forward with hesitancy, wondering where, in all this confusing blackness, she could find refuge when, at a turn in the road, she came suddenly upon a small public-house, its painted sign swinging disconsolately in the wind, one naked light showing above the shabby saloon door. Sabina knew little of public-houses, but she imagined that all and every one of them must have rooms to let. If the landlady was kind . . . if they would trust her until tomorrow . . . The ticket-collector's reaction had not been encouraging, but perhaps

12

he had been slow to understand; in any case it was no fit night to wander aimlessly in a strange countryside. Sabina walked round the solitary car which' stood outside and, gathering her courage together, pushed open the saloon door.

It was a quiet little bar and rather shabby. A man stood behind the counter in his shirtsleeves staring morosely into a glass of bitter; the only customer sat on a stool in the corner, his hat pulled down over his eyes to meet the upturned collar of his raincoat.

"Yes, miss?" the landlord said without enthusiasm.

"I—I want a room for the night," Sabina said, approaching the bar uncertainly.

"Don't let rooms," the man said laconically. "What'll you have?"

"I don't want anything to drink, thank you. I just wanted a room," Sabina said a little desperately.

The landlord finished his beer and wiped his mouth with the back of his hand.

"I've told you, we don't let rooms," he said and added, eyeing her suspiciously, "You got a car?"

"No," said Sabina, surprised.

"Then where's your luggage?"

She began to tell him, but at the expression in his eyes she faltered and came to a stop.

"Is there anyone else round here who would take me in?" she ventured at last.

"No," he replied, "and if you take my tip you won't try that hard-luck story in these parts. Cornish folk are suspicious of foreigners—specially them without luggage *or* money at this time of night."

Sabina bit her lip, trying to keep back the tears.

"I'm not a foreigner," she said, defending the only item in his accusations which she felt to be unjustified.

The stranger at the other end of the bar spoke for the first time.

"The term doesn't imply what you think. It simply means you are not a native of these parts. You might at least serve the young lady with a drink on this filthy night, landlord, even if she hasn't any money. I'll pay."

Sabina turned to look at him, disturbed by the harshness of his voice and the unexpected intrusion into her affairs. His face was in shadow, but she got the impression of pronounced features and a dark complexion.

"No, thank you," she said, "I—I don't drink much."

"Very right and proper. What'll it be?"

The landlord regarded her with weary resignation.

"Come off it, lady," he said. "I don't belong to these parts, neither. I'm familiar with such tales where I come from. Might as well get something for your trouble since you've found a gent to oblige."

Sabina said nothing, hating them both, aware now that she was tired and hungry and that running away had been a mistake from the start.

"Brandy," the stranger said a little sharply, and when the drink was bought, carried it with his own to the far end of the bar as if to exclude the landlord from further conversation.

"You'd better take the next stool," he said, and Sabina could do no less than comply.

She sat beside him, twining her legs nervously round the long legs of the stool, and stared down at the small glass of brandy in awkward silence.

"Aren't you going to drink it?" her companion inquired, and she detected mockery in his voice.

She picked up her glass and took a good gulp, which made her cough. Tante liked her *fine* after dinner, but brandy to Sabina had usually meant hot milk and sickness.

"You've been badly brought up, or have you got your eye on the clock for closing time?" the stranger said.

She did not understand him and took another gulp to evade answering.

"Dear me!" he remarked mildly. "You'd better bring another, landlord; your optic must give short measure."

"And what do you mean by that, sir?" demanded the landlord belligerently.

"It was a jest," the stranger replied equably. "Never think that we should be questioning your hospitality."

Sabina giggled with the consoling impression that they were both in league against the disagreeable landlord, but when the second brandy was slapped down in front of her she regarded it dubiously.

"Oh, I don't think—" she began, but the stranger observed carelessly:

"Two will do you good, but make this one last, please. Brandy—even the stuff dished out in English pubs—is not meant to be taken at a draught."

She felt reproved and, glancing at him sideways, relinquished the impression that he was somehow on her side. He had removed his hat, and his face, revealed fully for the first time, was not reassuring. He had a slightly saturnine look, she thought, with black eyebrows that lifted at the corners and a hard, twisted mouth. His hair was black and very thick, and his eyes, when he turned unexpectedly to regard her, were a cold, clear blue, disconcerting and somehow alien in his dark face.

"Well, you've had a good look—now it's my turn," he said, but she averted her face, embarrassed that he had caught her staring, and was immediately confronted with her own reflection in the fly-blown mirror behind the bar. It was a discouraging face, she reflected mournfully, very conscious of his eyes on her profile. The pointed chin and high, rounded forehead did not seem balanced by eyes that were too large and too widely spaced. The fine, pale hair, still damp from the rain, brushed her shoulders in unfashionable disorder, and her cheek-bones, as Tante had often told her, were too pronounced.

She sighed and he said with a sudden disarming warmth: "Tell me how you've come to be stranded."

The brandy had given her the courage to confide.

"I've run away," she said and his eyebrows rose.

"From school?"

"Oh, no, I've finished with school. From my aunt and Marthe and from—" She paused.

"And from who else?"

"The man I'm going to marry."

"Indeed. You are engaged, then?"

"Well, not exactly, but Tante has arranged matters."

"Tante? But you are not French."

"Oh, no. Tante is my aunt by marriage, and she prefers to be addressed in the French manner—she *is* French, of course."

"And why do you run away from this man you say you are to marry?"

"Because—well, I don't know that I can really explain. I'm not running away from *him*, exactly, though I think

15

he's an elderly *roué*, but—well, I suppose it was what Tante would call a *crise de nerfs,* only I'm not supposed to suffer from that."

"I see. And your—fiancé—does he understand about *crises de nerfs?*"

"I don't know," said Sabina simply, "I've never met him."

*   *   *

As soon as she had spoken she realised that she had been misled by a warmth which did not exist. The stranger's eyes held a chill appraisal and the corner of his mouth had a cynical twist.

"You don't believe me?" she faltered, and he gave the suspicion of a shrug which reminded her of Tante.

"It doesn't sound very likely, does it?" he replied. "A fiancé you have never met and an unknown destination in Cornwall. What are you really running away from, or is our friend the landlord by any chance right and this is just a rather ingenuous story?"

Sabina raised her pointed chin.

"I've told you the truth," she said with dignity, "or at least a part of it. There were other reasons, too, that made me come to Cornwall."

"I'm sure there were," he countered dryly. "But I should think up something less dated for your next attempt."

"Dated?" she repeated blankly. The brandy and the closeness of the little bar were making her feel sleepy.

"Well, in this year of grace girls are not married off by their relations to unknown suitors. What old-fashioned trash have you been reading?"

"In France they are," said Sabina, and he frowned.

"But we are not in France. What do you plan as your next move?"

Sabrina felt suddenly isolated. She was conscious of the two men waiting for her reply and of the slow, loud ticking of the clock on the wall. Rain still beat against the windows and somewhere a dog barked once.

When she did not answer the uncomfortable stranger said with a hint of impatience:

"Well, where are you trying to get to? At least you must know that."

"Oh, yes," she replied with relief. "I was going to a place called Truan, but the last train will have gone by now."

"In that case I can give you a lift in my car," he said smoothly. "It happens that I'm going to Truan myself. Your friends will doubtless straighten out the matter of the lost purse and luggage tomorrow."

"My friends?"

"If your story is true, presumably someone is expecting you."

"No . . . no, they aren't . . ." she said guiltily, and saw the scepticism back in his chilly regard.

"Then where were you proposing to stop?" he asked and sounded suddenly bored with the whole affair.

"I thought—at the village inn—unless it's like this one and doesn't let rooms," she said timidly.

"Whether it does or not, you will scarcely be welcomed at this hour of night with no luggage and no money. Really, my dear young lady, I'm hanged if I know whether you're as simple as you sound or not very bright at making a touch."

"A touch?" It was a new expression to Sabina, but the landlord enlightened her, winking at his other customer as he did so.

"Putting on the screws—or as the cops would have it, obtaining money under false pretences," he said, and Sabina flushed scarlet.

"*Oh!*" she cried, knocking over her unfinished brandy as she slithered off the stool and made blindly for the door.

Almost at once she felt a hand grip her shoulder with uncompromising firmness and turned to find the stranger beside her.

"Not so fast," he said softly. "I'm inclined to think we've misjudged you, after all."

"Speak for yourself," snapped the landlord sourly. "But whatever larks you like to get up to with the young person, you'll do it off these premises. It's closing time."

They left the public-house together, the stranger's hand still firmly gripping Sabina's shoulder, as if he knew all about that instinct of hers to run off again into the darkness. They stood outside in the rain and heard the land-lord bolt the door behind them. The light over the door went out suddenly and Sabina was afraid. Marthe's warnings about strange men came back to point a horrid lesson in regard to truancy, and in the darkness her com-panion appeared very tall and alarming. He made her no easier by remarking a little grimly:

"Whatever the truth of the matter may be, you are not a very wise young woman to confide preposterous stories to a perfect stranger. Now you'll have to accept that lift to Truan."

She pulled away from him, but his fingers tightened on her shoulder.

"No, you don't," he said. "If your story is true, you need help of a kind, and, if you're having me on, the sooner you're sent back to where you belong the better. In either case I can't very well leave you standing in the rain on a cold winter's night. There's my car. Get in."

There was no alternative. She waited wretchedly while he opened the door of the car, noticing that he limped as he walked; then she got in without speaking, and the treacherous tears overflowed at last. If he observed that she was crying he made no comment as he got in beside her and drove away. She sat as far from him as was possible, convinced now that at her very first bid for free-dom she had fallen into the hands of an unscrupulous despoiler, but he took no notice of her, and presently her tears ceased and she was conscious only of a great wear-iness and the forlorn hope that this was merely a contin-uation of her dream in the train.

The roads were narrow and the banks high. Every so often there was a break in the banks and wild, uninhabit-ed country seemed to lie beyond, but it was too dark to see much and rain blurred window and windscreen alike.

Her companion spoke suddenly, making her jump.

"I don't take advantage of children, you know, how-ever opportune the situation," he said with a hint of laughter in his voice.

She made an effort to recapture her adult dignity.

"That relieves me," she replied with polite gravity, "but I'm not a child. I'm nineteen."

"Indeed? And contemplating a marriage of convenience

with—an elderly *roué*, I think you called him."

"But you didn't believe me."

"Well, perhaps you haven't made the situation very clear. Suppose you try to explain all over again. We have fifteen miles or so to drive, and it will pass the time."

He was only humouring her, she knew, but her fear of him had gone. With the landlord's unpleasant company removed, perhaps she could convince him.

She began at the beginning with Tante's adoption of her, sketching in the confused details of her upbringing with careful exactitude.

"It was not that they wished me to be lonely, you must understand," she said, "but there was not much money, and Tante naturally felt cheated because the house could not be sold."

"The house?"

"Yes, I own a house, but Tante discovered too late it was entailed in trust for my—my children—and of course that made things difficult for everybody."

He gave her a swift glance. Unless she had a very lively imagination it seemed scarcely likely that she should be inventing this detail for his edification.

"Yes, I understand your aunt's disillusionment," he observed dryly. "And how does the elderly suitor come into the story?"

"Oh, on account of the house. It really belongs in his family, and the only way he can get it back is by taking me with it, Tante says. You see, it suits all round. Tante wants to get me off her hands and have—security for her old age, and the house could be useful to *him*, while it's a white elephant to *us*, so—it seemed the simplest way out. Don't you agree?"

"Very neat and tidy. There's only one loose end. How do you know, if you've never met him, that your elderly *roué* is willing to marry a stranger, even if you are?"

"Tante has arranged matters," she replied. "Only yesterday she went to France to make the final arrangements."

"To France! Is it a French family you are about to marry into, then?"

He spoke sharply, and she answered with apology.

"Oh, yes. Didn't I make that clear? I wouldn't suppose,

19

as you pointed out, that an Englishman would be so obliging as to marry a girl he had never met."

There was a long silence, and she could sense his change of mood, though whether he was still sceptical or merely disinterested she had no means of knowing.

At last he asked: "What's the name of this house you say you own?"

"Penruthan. It's near this village, Truan, where we are going. That was the real reason I ran away," she added shyly. "I've never seen it and—well, I suppose that shouldn't make any difference, really, but I wanted to get there first."

"Penruthan . . ." he repeated slowly and she inquired with interest if he knew the place.

"Yes, " he said. "This isn't my first visit to Truan, you know. Penruthan is quite a landmark in these parts."

He began to slow down, and presently he stopped the car on the side of a moorland road and lit a cigarette. He did not offer one to Sabina, and appeared to have forgotten her.

Her doubts returned as she sat beside him listening to the wind and the rain. They seemed to be miles from anywhere, and nothing had passed them on the road.

"Why have you stopped?" she asked, and he replied absently:

"Not for the reason you suppose. Tell me, what's the name of this Frenchman who wants your house?"

"René Bergerac. He has a hotel. I believe it's quite famous."

"René Bergerac . . ."

"Have you heard of him, too?" she asked, no longer surprised that on this unpredictable evening coincidence should make a bond between herself and this stranger.

"Naturally, anyone who has visited France has heard the name of René Bergerac—the father at any rate, if not the son."

He spoke with the now familiar dryness, and she said, like a child caught out in a gross invention:

"Now I suppose you believe me less than ever."

"On the contrary," he replied, flinging away his half-smoked cigarette, "it might even begin to make a little sense."

"You know M. Bergerac, perhaps?"

He smiled without humour.

"In a sense I suppose I do. What gives you the idea that he's an elderly *roué*?"

"Things that Tante and Marthe have said, I suppose," she answered, and added politely: "I'm sorry if I have hurt your feelings."

"Why should you hurt my feelings?" he retorted unsympathetically, and she realised he was angry. "It's not I you think of in such unflattering terms, though I fancy up till this moment you had reservations about my intentions. And what of the good Marthe? Won't she take fright at your disappearance and communicate immediately with Madame?"

"Not tonight, anyway. She is visiting her friend in Hampstead, and when she comes back she will find my note explaining."

"And tomorrow?"

"I had not thought as far as tomorrow," she faltered, and his smile was a little sardonic.

"Bad generalship?" he remarked. "For tonight, then, you'd better come home with me."

"Home . . . with you?"

In the dim glow from the dashboard he could see her astonished eyes widen to such an extent that her pale, small face seemed to shrink visibly.

"Now don't get other ideas," he said hastily. "It's not really my home. I'm on a visit to my old governess. She's the widow of the late vicar of Truan and very respected."

"But she won't be expecting you to bring a stranger so late at night."

His eyebrows lifted still higher at the corners, accentuating that fleeting satanic likeness he possessed as he said:

"Ah, but you see, a parson's wife learns to give shelter to the needy; nothing ever surprises her; also she happens to be quite fond of me."

He spoke lightly, but she knew he was still angry, either with her or at the inconvenience to himself. She sat there blinking at him, aware that she had no choice but to agree and that, whatever the outcome of this adventure, she was too tired to argue.

"Well, if you really think—" she began doubtfully, and he restarted his engine.

"I think on the whole it was lucky you ran into me and not another type of pub-crawler at this hour of the night," he observed caustically. "Tomorrow we'll see about retrieving your missing belongings."

He had accepted her story. In the happiness which came with relief, she felt an overwhelming sense of gratitude towards him.

"Thank you," she said shyly. "Don't—don't you want to know my name?"

"Your name? Oh, yes. What is your name?"

"Sabina. Sabina Lamb." He made no immediate comment, and she thought he had not heard her and repeated her name again.

"A lamb being led to the slaughter, or a fairly complacent victim?" he said, but if he meant it as a joke she did not respond.

"I've grown up with the idea," she replied gently. "Only I wish sometimes he was stronger."

"An invalid as well as a *roué?*"

"N-no," she said doubtfully. "But I think his digestion is weak."

He grunted non-committally, and they sat there in silence with the engine of the car gently turning over, and Sabina said:

"You know my name, btu you haven't told me yours."

"Haven't I?" he answered absently. "It's Brockman— I'm called Brock for short. We'd better be getting on or Bunny will have given me up. Are you warm enough?" he added as he saw her shiver.

"Yes, thank you, but I'm a little damp," she said; then fell asleep before they had covered the next couple of miles.

CHAPTER TWO

SHE awoke, feeling stiff and feverish, as the car slowed down through the village, and rubbed a circle on the misted window to look out.

"Is this Truan?" she asked, gazing with surprise at the few dark cottages. She supposed there was a shop and a post-office, but there seemed to be no village street in the usual sense, and the little inn stood on a tiny square of grass and looked hardly big enough to house anyone but the landlord and his wife.

"Is that the only inn?" Sabina asked, wondering what she should do on the morrow when she would have to leave the hospitality of the unknown governess's roof.

"Yes," Brock replied. "And you wouldn't have found a room there, either. Your sudden flight would have seemed inadvisable without making proper inquiries."

She felt reproved once more, but in her ignorance she had supposed all village inns welcomed the traveller with an ever open door. She had stayed very little in the country.

The rectory stood alone on the edge of the moor, a long, sprawling house with a jutting wing so thickly covered with ivy that it was difficult to see the windows. The churchyard encroached upon the rough garden but there was no church.

Sabina stood shivering in the wind while Brock took his suitcases from the back of the car, and stared at the graves so uncomfortably near the house.

Brock observed the direction of her gaze and remarked with grim dryness:

"Very salutary living close to the dead."

"Is it?" she replied with polite uncertainty, and he told her impatiently to ring the bell.

"There are no ghosts here, but it looks as though Bunny has given me up and gone to bed," he said.

Sabina tugged at the iron handle in the porch and heard a bell echoing faintly somewhere at the back of the house. By now she would be unsurprised at however the day might end, but when presently the heavy door was opened and lamplight and the scent of burning wood came to meet her, she knew only that she was very tired, that shivers ran up and down her spine which had nothing to do with the silent graves outside, and that wherever she had found herself, a warm bed would be the greatest benison of all.

A small, neat woman stood in the doorway, peering out. Even in the dim light, she had the authentic air of an old-fashioned governess, with her netted hair and high-necked bodice and pince-nez suspended from a button by a fine chain, but her voice, when she spoke, though precise, held a youthful eagerness.

"Brock . . . is that you?"

She did not see Sabina, pressed against the wall of the porch, and as Brock gathered her up into a warm embrace, Sabina felt herself to be an intruder.

"My dear boy, how glad I am to see you," Bunny said, automatically patting her hair back into place. "I had almost given you up, and although there have been hot bottles in your bed all day, they must be cold now, and Tregenna has never been to mend that catch on your window."

"Dear Bunny," Brock said, and Sabina was surprised by the simple affection in his voice. "It might have been only yesterday that you saw me, instead of a year ago. Haven't you had that catch dealt with yet?"

"Nobody uses that room but you," Bunny said. "I should have remembered. But come into the warm, dear boy. Was it the weather that delayed you?"

"No, not entirely," he said. "I've brought another guest for the night, Bunny. I hope it won't be too much trouble to fix up a room. Come out of your retirement, young lady, and meet our Bunny, who has always had a welcome for everyone."

Sabina advanced uncertainly into the circle of light, but she did not think the welcome of Brock's governess extended so universally as he imagined. Bunny surveyed her shrewdly, and there was reservation in her voice and a gentle air of reproof as she said:

"Could you not have let me know, Brock? There are no fires lighted in the other rooms and the beds are not aired."

"I'm sorry, my dear," Brock answered with rather puckish enjoyment, "but I hadn't met the young lady myself until a couple of hours ago. This is Miss Sabina Lamb. She has run away from a rich fiancé she has never met and has lost her purse and her luggage on the way."

Bunny gave him a long look.

"Have you been drinking?" she asked with mild severity.

"No," he replied quite seriously. "I called for a quick one on the road, where I met our runaway. In the circumstances I could do nothing else but bring her with me. Will you ask us in, Bunny dear? Your guest has an aversion to the graveyard."

"Of course, of course," Bunny said, annoyed that surprise should have made her appear lacking in hospitality, but she added a little reprovingly as she closed the door: "A graveyard should not be shunned by the living. We all have to come to it."

Sabina, chilled by the reminder, stood in the shadowy hall, feeling lost and alien. She was unused to lamplight and the peculiar stillness of a country house. The shadows played tricks with her unaccustomed eyes and she knew that she was unwanted by these two strangers upon whom fate had so perversely thrust her. She became aware that the governess had picked up one of the small oil lamps and was inspecting her more closely in the light. She had placed her pince-nez on her long pinched nose and through them her round brown eyes observed with the deliberate summing up of her profession. She was really rather like a rabbit, Sabina thought uneasily, with her round mild eyes and slightly protuberant teeth.

"Why, she's only a child," Bunny said then, and for some reason her voice sounded sharp and impatient.

"Nineteen, so she tells me," Brock observed, watching with amusement, "but that can be an age of much knowledge these sophisticated days."

Bunny gave him a disapproving look, and the lenses of her pince-nez flashed in the light as she set the lamp down again.

"If I didn't know you better, Brock——" she began, and he grinned.

"How well do you think you know me?" he interrupted. "Miss Sabina Lamb has been convinced for some time past of my base designs, haven't you, Sabina?"

"Then she should know better than to accompany a perfect stranger to an unknown destination even if she has lost her luggage," said Bunny tartly, but as she saw the girl began to sway a little on her feet she turned her back firmly on Brock.

"What am I thinking of!" she exclaimed. "You look exhausted, child, and feverish, too, if I'm not mistaken. Come into the living-room and sit by the fire while I get you both some hot soup."

Sabina followed her into a room on the right of the hall and sank thankfully on to a wooden settle by the fire. She had never seen such a vast open hearth before. The chimney was like a cavern and you could roast an ox with ease, she thought. The room was long and low-ceilinged, and smoke had turned the whitewash between the beams to a dusty yellow. There was a great deal of furniture and numerous little tables bearing framed snapshots of children; brass and copper and odd and often hideous pieces of china decorated the walls, and a great *armoire* of exquisite workmanship and proportions rubbed shoulders with a cheap cabinet from which the paint was peeling. It was an extraordinary room to Sabina's eyes, accustomed to the stereotyped modernity of small hotels, and tired though she was, she longed to pry further into the shadows, and explore the dark corners filled with so many unusual things.

Brock watched her as he warmed his back by the fire.

"Does the room shock you?" he inquired with derisive amusement. "It's hardly evidence of a collector's taste, is it?"

"Why should it shock me?" she asked simply. "I wouldn't know about collectors' tastes, anyway. I—I like it."

"So do I," he agreed surprisingly. "Bunny occupies each room in the house in strict rotation when she's alone, but her personal favourites are here."

"And it's where they should be," said Bunny briskly, coming into the room with two bowls of soup on a tray. "This is the heart of the house, and I don't expect or

26

need the approval of the young of today. I'm old-fashioned, and don't mind who knows it."

"Sabina must be old-fashioned, too," said Brock with his customary dryness. "She is a dutiful niece ready to be forced into marriage with an elderly *roué* at her aunt's command."

Bunny's quick eyes saw the suspicious brightness on Sabina's lashes and she said reprovingly:

"What nonsense are you talking? Here we both are snapping at the poor child, and whatever the reason for her presence here she looks fit to drop."

Sabina was at the stage of exhaustion when a few kind words would be her undoing, and Bunny hastily placed a bowl of soup on a stool beside her and bade her drink it at once.

"I should explain," Sabina began between scalding mouthfuls which made her eyes water in earnest, "I should try to explain why I'm here at all."

"The explanation, though hard to swallow, is very enlightening," Brock said softly, and Bunny gave him a quick look.

"Explanations can wait till the morning," she said with firmness. "Miss Lamb has a temperature, if I'm not mistaken. I shall go and put a hot bottle in one of the beds at once. The room will be cold, as there's only a fire lighted in yours, Brock, but it can't he helped."

"She'd better have mine for tonight, then," he said indifferently. "If she's got a chill we don't want her any worse by morning."

The governess compressed her lips, then nodded.

"Perhaps that would be best," she said, but it was clear that she considered the intrusion most unfortunate. It was not for a strange young girl she had prepared with loving care the room which no one but Brock ever used.

Sabina tried to protest, but they took no notice of her, and Brock observed with his twisted smile:

"You needn't think we're being unselfish, my dear; neither of us is anxious for a sick guest on our hands tomorrow."

"That wasn't kind," Bunny reproved. "Miss Lamb is my guest at any rate for tonight, and you should know better by now than to embarrass someone under your own roof."

But he looked unrepentant, and Sabina, following her hostess across the hall and up a flight of dark, slippery stairs, resolved that however she felt by the morning she would relieve them both of her presence as early as possible.

Brock's room, unlike the one downstairs, was high and uncluttered. The furniture was solid and masculine and the books, in a glass-fronted bookcase, well bound and selected with discrimination. The walls were hung with very fine photographs of mountain peaks and ranges. They lent an austere and strangely impersonal air to the room, as if the high places of the earth could have no part in the mundane affairs of man. Sabina suspected that Brock himself had supervised the arrangements for this room, and she wished, in spite of the welcoming peat fire, that she could have slept elsewhere. She did not want to be reminded of the inconvenience she had caused him.

Bunny had left her to fetch what might be required for the night, and she returned now with a few necessities and laid an old-fashioned nightdress carefully on the bed.

"Not what you're used to, no doubt, but it will serve," she said, and Sabina experienced a wild desire to laugh.

The nightdress was of flannelette with long sleeves gathered at the wrists and a high buttoned neck finished modestly with feather-stitching. She could hear Tante exclaiming with horror: *"Mon dieu, c'est incroyable!"*

"The bathroom is next door. There is a nightlight there, but mind the steps," Bunny said, casting a last practised glance about the room. "If you are not accustomed to an oil lamp don't touch it except to blow it out. They smitch very easily."

"Smitch?"

"Smoke. It's a west-country expression. Good night, my dear, and I hope you'll feel better in the morning."

"Thank you. Good night, Miss—Miss Bunny, and I'm sorry to be such a trouble," said Sabina and immediately blushed. Of course Brock's ex-governess was no longer "Miss," neither was her surname Bunny. A faint smile touched Bunny's rather prim mouth but she made no correction. She observed the blush with interest and quietly left the room and went downstairs.

Sabina stood in the middle of the big room and tried to find fresh amusement in contemplating the nightdress. But the nightdress no longer seemed funny. It looked more like a shroud than a relic of Edwardian propriety, and, remembering the graves so close beneath her window, Sabina sat down on the floor and wept with sudden desolation.

*　　*　　*

Morning brought no relief to the situation and for Sabina the unhappy knowledge that, however unwilling, she must trespass further on this grudging hospitality, for she had been sick all night, falling repeatedly down the bathroom steps despite Bunny's warning, and when daylight came she was weak and tearful and the fever of the night before had mounted.

"I must get Dr. Northy to have a look at her," Bunny told Brock when they met at breakfast. "I don't think it's more than a chill and possibly some sort of emotional disturbance, but the girl's a stranger to us. We cannot run any risks."

Brock's frown was dark and brooding, reminding her of those bitter weeks after his accident.

"I shouldn't have brought her here," he said, "but she was virtually stranded and, discounting the preposterous yarn she spun me at first, she really didn't seem very fit to fend for herself."

"The preposterous yarn presumably had something to do with the nonsense you were talking last night," Bunny observed. "Had she invented some tall story in order to get free lodging for the night?"

"I thought so at first, but later—well, she produced some rather startling facts which can be verified or not. What did you make of her?"

"A nice child, I think," she replied after a pause. "I felt more sure of her as soon as she blushed."

"As soon as she blushed?" His eyebrows went up, but he remembered at the same time Sabina's vivid blush at the landlord's comments in the little public-house at Kairy. "What had you been saying to her, Bunny?"

"When she said good night she addressed me as Miss Bunny and then went scarlet with embarrassment. The young don't blush any more, Brock. When you find one that does there is usually something tender and vulnerable about them."

"You think so? Yet this girl, if she is to be believed, is quite ready to marry a man whom she has never seen and whom she doesn't appear to have very flattering ideas about."

She looked across at him with the tolerant expression with which he had been familiar in his boyhood.

'Perhaps you had better try to explain," she said. "Who, in any case, are Tante and Marthe? The girl isn't French."

"No. Tante is aunt by marriage, I imagine. She apparently had expectations through the niece that couldn't be realised, so wants to marry her off."

"Expectations? Is the girl an heiress, then?" Bunny's voice was dry. Sabina's clothes had presented no evidence that thought had been spent on her wardrobe, neither had she given the impression of someone used to money.

Brock buttered a piece of toast with careful deliberation.

"She owns a house which is unfortunately entailed—a useless asset when it boils down to hard cash," he said, and she looked at him inquiringly.

"It still doesn't make much sense—unless, of course, the aunt has someone up her sleeve who wants the house enough to take the girl with it."

"She has. Sabina is the owner of Penruthan. Strange, isn't it?"

"Penruthan . . ." Bunny sat up very straight and stiff in her chair, her round eyes suddenly shrewd. "But that means . . . Brock! You wouldn't encourage—you wouldn't permit—"

His bitter smile was cynical.

Marriage with an elderly *roué* with a weak digestion? My advice hasn't been asked, rather naturally, my dear, and I, a stranger, am scarcely in the position to offer any, am I?"

"In a very good position, I should have said," Bunny retorted, but she looked disturbed. "How long have you known of this—this curious arrangement, Brock?"

"Since last night."

"Only last night! Then——"

"What else were you thinking?" He was mocking her. "Should I have said immediately: 'My poor child, the son of René Bergerac is not for you. Tell your aunt to make other arrangements'?"

"It's preposterous!" Bunny exclaimed.

"But typically French," Brock reminded her gently. Her small mouth set in stubborn lines.

"You should tell her the truth."

"Come now, Bunny, that might be embarrassing for all concerned. One needs a little more confirmation——on both sides."

"Then we must send her back where she belongs as soon as she is fit to travel. The affair is distasteful and—— awkward. Unless——"

"Unless what?"

"There's another side," she answered lamely. It was not quite what had been in her mind, but she knew Brock of old when he chose to sit on the fence and intervene only when it suited him.

"There's always another side," he said, knowing exactly what she was thinking. "And as for sending the child back to where she belongs, it may interest you to know that her aunt has already gone to the Château Berger to bring matters to a head."

"And you believe that?"

"I've no reason to doubt it. But one can get corroboration from the good Marthe, who, incidentally, must be in quite a state by now, not knowing where her charge is. You had better get the London address and wire her, Bunny. I, for my part, will try to trace the missing luggage."

Bunny rose at once and went upstairs. She was angry with Brock for becoming involved in an affair so outrageously foreign, and with Sabina for crossing his path at such a moment. It was possible, of course, that the girl had invented the whole thing, either to make an impression or for uglier reasons of her own, but when she stood beside the bed and looked down at the small, pointed face with its delicate bones, Bunny found it difficult to preserve her suspicions. The child was painfully thin in the bright light of morning and when she opened her eyes they held apology and acute embarrassment.

"I'm so sorry to be such a nuisance," she said. "I think I could get up and get dressed now, though. I haven't been sick for a long time."

"Not until the doctor has seen you. He'll be here this morning," Bunny replied, but without sympathy.

Sabina was conscious of a new resentment behind the woman's precise manner.

"I had better go back to London and Marthe," she said with an air of defeat.

"Without a return ticket or any money?"

"I'd forgotten. Where should I inquire to try to get them back?"

"Mr. Brockman is doing it for you. In the meantime he thinks we should let this Marthe know where you are. Will you let me have her full name and address, please?"

"Oh, dear, she will be angry."

"Did you not think of that when you ran away, my dear?"

"Oh, yes, but it seemed worth it then for a—a few days' freedom."

"It is never worth upsetting other people and causing anxiety," Bunny observed in her best lecture manner. "If she has been left in charge while your aunt is abroad it was hardly kind or thoughtful to think only of yourself, was it?"

"No, I suppose not, only—"

"Well, I shouldn't try to think of excuses now. I will do my best to assure the woman you are in good hands. Please give me her name and address."

Sabina did so humbly. She was oppressed with her own iniquity and the trouble she was causing to strangers. Tante, if she knew, would accuse her of ingratitude, but Tante, if she returned with M. Bergerac, as hoped, could this time be placated. It was foolish, she thought with passing surprise at her own temerity, to run away from a future already accepted.

Bunny observed her dispassionately. The feverish flush which heightened her cheek-bones gave the girl's face an impression of fragile charm which it had lacked last night, and the rounded forehead was child-like and somehow disarming. In other circumstances, Bunny felt she could have approved, and even been sorry that such an innocent should be sacrificed to the selfish whims of others. She did relax sufficiently to bestow a brief, frosty smile on her guest before leaving her to make the necessary arrangements, but Sabina was not reassured. Bunny did not like her, it was clear, and Mr. Brockman, already regretting his kindly action of yesterday, no doubt, must also be anxious to be rid of any further responsibility. She turned on her side and slipped into a doze until the doctor came.

When Brock returned at lunch-time, having recovered Sabina's lost property without much trouble, he was greeted by Bunny in a familiar mood.

"You must be prepared, my dear boy, to suffer a little further inconvenience on account of your hasty decision yesterday," she said. "Dr. Northy says the girl is not fit to travel for a day or two and needs rest and quiet and feeding up. He thinks she has been under an emotional strain and hasn't had enough to eat. He has a weakness for the very young."

"So?"

"So, she must remain here, naturally, until she is stronger. But I'm afraid we shall have this woman, Marthe Dupont, to contend with as well. I thought it best to put a call through and explain, rather than send a mystifying telegram. She was very voluble and French, and, I think, highly suspicious. She insists on coming down on the afternoon train and taking charge herself."

"Oh, Lord, Bunny, I'm sorry," Brock said, frowning impatiently. "As if you hadn't got enough on your hands as it is, but still—the woman's a trained servant, I gather, perhaps she can relieve you of some of the work."

"Perhaps," said Bunny with a dubious smile. "Though, from what I know of other people's servants, they are seldom anxious to do their share in a strange house. Still, it cannot be helped. She can at least look after the girl and carry up trays."

Brock frowned again.

"She's not really ill, is she? After all, this house isn't a nursing home."

"No, no—just run down and suffering from a chill. My only regret is that it interferes with your visit. A year is a long time since your last little holiday, and I think you need the rest. Does your leg trouble you much these days?"

"The physical discomfort is less irksome than the spiritual," he replied impatiently, and she gave him a compassionate glance.

"Still hankering for the mountains?" she asked. "Well, they tell us that discipline is good for the soul. You must learn acceptance, Brock."

His eyes were cold and a little bleak.

"Haven't the last few years taught me that?"

"I'm not sure. There's been nothing to take the place of your earlier love."

"Meaning, I suppose, that if I'd found a desirable wife my passion for the mountains would be sublimated?"

She smiled, then compressed her lips.

"I don't set much store by such loose modern jargon," she said, "but there are other ways of fulfilling oneself besides climbing unconquerable heights and leading expeditions."

"You say that rather as if you thought such ambitions were merely an adult form of showing off."

"Not in your case," she answered seriously, "not in that of any of the real pioneers, but a physical infirmity should not embitter the spirit. There are other ways of fulfilment."

He moved abruptly, dragging his stiff limb with unconscious impatience.

"So you said," he returned shortly, then dismissed the subject altogether. "You don't have to put up with this Frenchwoman here, you know. We can probably find her a room in the village."

"She won't trouble me," said Bunny serenely. "Also, I think it might be a good opportunity to find out a little more about this matter."

"With discretion," Brock said, one eyebrow lifted quizzically.

She gave him a reproving look.

"Naturally," she said. "Only I think you must make your intentions—if indeed you have any—a little clearer to me, first. But that can wait; luncheon, I think, is ready."

*   *   *

Marthe arrived in the evening and at once made her presence felt in the house. Although she came of peasant stock she had spent all her life in cities, and one glance at the shabby country rectory and the dowdy little woman who greeted her prosaically, although assuring her of propriety, confirmed her worst fears of English discomfort.

She sat in the kitchen drinking, without gratitude, the soup which Bunny had prepared for her, and appraised Brock in silence out of her small, pig-like eyes.

She had been unprepared for Brock, who had met her at the station, and was disturbed to find that he was also stopping in the house. Accustomed to Tante's sleek, well-tailored escorts, she found nothing to admire in the worn slacks and faded pullover which this tall man wore with the negligent casualness of a peasant, but Sabina, she thought, had led too sheltered a life to be as discerning, and it was possible that an escapade such as last night's might give her notions which Madame could find very upsetting to her plans.

"You will observe the usual rules in my absence," Tante had said upon departure. "The child is prepared against eventualities. I want no foolish distractions to interfere now—no adolescent infatuations or imagined friendships. You understand?"

Marthe had understood perfectly. She had not thought, herself, there was danger from outside influences, for Sabina had no opportunities for making friends of her own and, in Marthe's opinion, no gift for attracting admiration. Yet now, in the space of twenty-four hours, she had run away, ventured into a public-house, and allowed a perfect stranger to take her home for the night.

Marthe's tightly encased bosom swelled as the enormity of the situation struck her, and the coarse black down on her long upper lip seemed to bristle as she announced suddenly:

"In case Mademoiselle failed to tell you, Monsieur, she is already promised."

Bunny surveyed the flat, sallow face with distaste, but Brock merely raised his eyebrows and replied mildly:

"Mademoiselle told me several odd things. Perhaps you can explain."

"I do not know, Monsieur, what Mademoiselle saw fit to tell you," Marthe retorted. "But that she is betrothed to a rich gentleman of France is true. Madame Lamb, my employer, is there at this moment concluding the negotiations."

"Negotiations?" repeated Brock.

Marthe gave him an appraising stare. Young, yes, by more mature standards, but too old to conform with a young girl's first dreams.

"You do not understand such things in this country," she said contemptuously. "But in France these matters are more sensibly arranged. Mademoiselle is to marry a man much respected and well able to provide for her—in the largest sense, you understand. Madame, her aunt, does not wish at this delicate state of the *affaire* that there should be—any distractions."

"And how delicate is the state of the *affaire*?" asked Brock, and Bunny gave him a quick, amused glance.

Marthe put down her empty bowl, and spread knees and hands in a familiar gesture of tolerance.

"It is only a matter of adjustment on both sides," she said. "But for Mademoiselle, you understand, it is a matter of duty. Madame has chosen the French way of settling the future. Mademoiselle has been brought up in that tradition and she does not, I assure you, wish for anything different."

Bunny had removed the soup bowl and was washing it up. She turned now to say over her shoulder:

"As you say, we do not understand such things very well in England, but how can you be sure that the method is wise? Miss Lamb is very young. It is possible that she might prefer to choose for herself."

"And where does it get one?" retorted Marthe with sardonic amusement. "Does one know at so tender an age what one wants? Are *you* happier for making your own choice, Madame?"

It was a shot in the dark, Bunny supposed, recognising the ridicule, but with the knowledge that her own marriage

36

had come too late in life to alter her obvious spinster status in anything but name, she had no reply.

"Mrs. Fennell is your hostess—personalities are not required of you. It would be as well, I think, if you went upstairs to Mademoiselle, and refrained, equally, from upsetting her unduly. She is not well, and needs rest and quiet for the next day or so."

Brock had spoken rapidly in French, and Marthe stood up instinctively, shocked into servitude as much by his sudden assumption of authority as the surprising flow of perfect French.

"I did not know you were so familiar with my tongue, Monsieur," she said ingratiatingly. "You speak as a Frenchman would. It is a pleasure to hear."

"Mrs. Fennell will take you upstairs," Brock observed. "In a day or so, we hope both you and Mademoiselle may return to London."

Bunny took Marthe to Sabina's room, speaking little on the way. She had taken an instant dislike to the insolent Frenchwoman and hoped it was not merely an insular prejudice. She was a humble creature, and knew only too well the average servant's opinion of a governess, but that Brock should be dismissed as of no account by this aggressive foreigner was more than she would tolerate. She had been touched and amused when he had asserted himself so unexpectedly.

The curtains were drawn and the lamp turned low in Sabina's room, and Bunny lingered deliberately to watch the meeting of these two.

"Well, mam'zelle, this is not a very pretty prank," Marthe said, standing at the foot of the bed with her hands on her broad hips.

Sabina raised an anxious face. She seemed better, but the colour was suddenly back in her cheek-bones and her eyes were apprehensive.

"I'm sorry, Marthe," she said. "I did not mean to lose my ticket and my luggage and oblige strangers to take me in."

"But you ran away," said Marthe. "You ran away when my back was turned, and now I cannot trust you out of my sight until Madame returns."

"It was only for a little while," Sabina pleaded. "I—I wanted to see the house."

"And could that not wait for M. Bergerac? The house is his concern, not yours."

"But it belongs to me."

"*Zut*! And what matter does that make? You have only caused trouble to everyone, and now are under the obligation to perfect strangers. Is that *gentil*? Is it, in any way, how you have been brought up?"

"I'm very happy to have Miss Lamb here," said Bunny unexpectedly. "And it is a misfortune rather than a crime to lose one's ticket and one's luggage."

Sabina shot her a surprised look of gratitude, but Marthe was not pleased.

"You are too amiable, madame," she said, without appreciation. "But Mademoiselle knows well her obligations. It is a matter which will displease Madame, her aunt, very deeply. You have forgotten, perhaps, mam'zelle, the sacrifices that have been made for you—the care that has been exercised for your future? You have, after all, the English ingratitude at heart and think only of yourself."

"No," said Sabina, and looked as if she were going to cry. "I did nothing wrong, Marthe . . . I only wanted to see my house . . . I didn't know that one could not stay at every village inn . . . if I had not lost my ticket . . ."

"If you had not lost your ticket, where in this uncivilised countryside would you have stayed?"

"I don't know," said Sabina wearily, and Bunny observed:

"Well, you are safe here at the rectory, so neither of you need speculate as to what might have happened. Marthe, Miss Lamb should settle down for the night, soon. Her temperature is still up and talking is not advised by the doctor."

Marthe turned to look at her. Removed from that shabbily dressed but disconcerting person downstairs, she was easily recognisable for what she was, and Marthe had no intention of relinquishing her supremacy in the sick room.

"Thank you madame, I do not need to be told the obvious," she said, her small eyes snapping. "Now, if you will please to leave us I will see that Mademoiselle has all she requires, after which I shall go to my own room if

38

you will be so civil as to acquaint me of its direction. I shall need hot-water bottles and a *tisane*, for this house is cold and you do not, I observe, have the central heating."

"You will find what you need in the kitchen," Bunny said a little sharply, and with a brief good night to Sabina, left the room.

Alone with Marthe, Sabina let her heavy lids fall, hoping to postpone the catechism that must follow, but Marthe would not leave her to sleep until she was fully satisfied.

"Who is this man?" she demanded. "And why is he here?"

"Mr. Brockman?" asked Sabina with surprise. "This is his home when he's on holiday."

"On holiday from what? What is his business?"

"I don't know. I haven't spoken to him since last night."

"Last night—when you allowed a stranger to bring you home—like any *demi-mondaine*."

"Oh, Marthe, it wasn't like that at all. He was only kind, as he would have been to any stray cat. He didn't even like me very much—neither does his governess."

"His governess!"

"Bunny—Mrs. Fennell—was once his governess. I think he spends his holidays with her."

Marthe began to laugh, relieved, but a little contemptuous. They did not know how to snatch the opportunities, these English *demoiselles*.

"As I thought," she said. "No background—no *panache* —the *bourgeois* young man who stays with the governess because, doubtless, he can afford nothing better. I can picture Madame's scorn; for a country gentleman, look you, has the tweeds most expensive and the handsome shoes and linen of the most impeccable. A country gentleman of wealth, she always says, you will know immediately by his clothes, for it is a fad of the British to affect the sporting at all times. And Madame, the governess—one can see at a glance that she has married above her station and too late in life. I have told them, of course, mam'zelle, that you are already promised."

Sabina opened her eyes. She thought that Marthe was probably talking a great deal of nonsense, but it was, she supposed, her method of warning Sabina to behave circumspectly until her future was resolved.

"I told them, too," she said. "Mr. Brockman seems to know or know of M. Bergerac."

Marthe frowned, remembering the fluent French which had momentarily so surprised her.

"That is possible," she replied carelessly. "If one has travelled, the name is well known, and M. Brockman is no stranger to France. He speaks the language like a native."

"Does he?" Sabina sounded surprised, then she added sleepily: "Then I can practise my own French while I'm here."

"You will not remain long enough," Marthe replied sharply, wondering if, after all, the girl had not cherished some romantic notions from this unexpected meeting.

"I suppose not," Sabina said indifferently, and her eyes closed again. Her head was aching and she wished Marthe would go away and leave her to sleep.

"*Alors*—you are tired," the woman said, speculating as to whether the unconcern was feigned or not. "I will leave you, for I, too, am tired. The journey was terrible, and this house—no lights, no heating and graves in the very garden! You will make haste and get well, mam'zelle, for I cannot stand many days of such an existence." At the door she paused to add with irritation: "The *toilette*—where it is?"

Having explained, Sabina had the satisfaction of hearing Marthe fall down the bathroom steps, just as she herself had done in the night, and the knowledge comforted her. Comfort came too from the fine snow-capped summits of Kanchenjunga, the nearest photograph on the wall by her bed. It was the last thing she remembered before she drifted into a dreamless sleep.

CHAPTER THREE

BUNNY found the Frenchwoman a perpetual irritant. Marthe would give no help in the house that was not concerned with her own and Sabina's welfare, and she refused to share the company in the kitchen of the daily woman who gave a few hours help in the mornings. She would sit by the fire in the living-room, complaining incessantly of draughts, and watch Bunny dust and polish with contemptuous indifference.

"Why do you not let the woman do this work?" she asked, regarding her hostess's efforts with a critical eye.

"This is a big house and she has enough to do in the time," Bunny replied, striving to be pleasant. "Besides, I don't care to idle, and it keeps my hand in for the summer."

Marthe grunted, a comment very French and very ambiguous, and Bunny felt bound to explain:

"In the summer I take a few paying guests; it all helps with the living expenses. Of course in the winter months no one comes to such a remote spot, and it's then I like to catch up with household chores."

"This an 'otel!" exclaimed Marthe with such scorn that Bunny had to smile.

"Well, scarcely that," she said. "I can only take two or three people at a time and we are too much off the beaten track for casual holiday-makers."

"And Monsieur, your husband, he reconciles such matters with his work in the parish?"

"My husband is dead," said Bunny quietly. The woman probably did not mean to be impertinent; she merely had the insatiable curiosity of her kind.

"*Pardon . . .*" Marthe muttered, then added irrespressibly: "But I see no church, only the graves which, look you, cannot be healthy so near at hand."

"The church is modern and up on the hill," Bunny replied. "After my husband died it was more convenient to build a smaller house close by for the new rector. The cemetery is here, yes, but in the Middle Ages the church was here, too. You can still see the ruins from the upstair windows. Perhaps you would be kind enough to give me a hand with this bookcase, Marthe. It is rather heavy to move alone."

The woman got up reluctantly. She did not see why M. Brockman, who appeared to have so much time on his hands, should not be summoned to make himself useful in such matters, or the imbecile boy who worked in the garden, but she half-heartedly helped Bunny shift the bookcase away from the wall and stood watching while a long-handled brush was thrust behind it to remove cobwebs.

"He is not strong, M. Brockman?" she hazarded.

"Perfectly, to the best of my knowledge."

"But one cannot help noticing the leg—it is an old war wound, *hein*?"

"No. It was an accident."

"*Tiens* . . . And Monsieur's business—it brings him here much?"

Bunny withdrew the brush and dusted her hands on her overall. She tied her head up in an unbecoming handkerchief while she was working and under it her face looked prim and pinched and rather absurd.

"Mr. Brockman is on holiday," she observed discouragingly. "You should ask him these things yourself, Marthe, if you are interested."

Marthe grunted again and returned to her seat by the fire, leaving her hostess to replace the bookcase as best she might. She recognised and resented the snub, knowing, as did Bunny, that she would not have the temerity to question Brock. She despised his shabbiness and the unconcern with which he would help with the evening washup, but there was a quality about him that made her uneasy. She kept a civil tongue when those frosty, dispassionate eyes were upon her, and when he spoke to her sharply in her own tongue she was not so sure in what category he might be placed.

"*M. le docteur* gives permission for us to return soon, yes?" she said, but Bunny shook her head.

"Miss Lamb is only getting up tomorrow for the first time," she said. "You will have to be patient for another few days, Marthe."

42

Bunny knew that Dr. Northy, who had also taken a dislike to Marthe, was prolonging the period of convalescence more than was necessary, but she had herself conceived a fondness for Sabina in the last few days. She did not care for the way Marthe spoke to the child, nor did she approve of the friendless life of neglect she appeared to lead in London.

Sabina had not asked for Brock, but on the third day, when her temperature was down again, he had gone upstairs to see her. She welcomed him doubtfully, very conscious that she had turned him out of his room for too long, and his expression as he stood at the foot of the bed, regarding her, was not reassuring.

"I'm afraid I've been a lot of trouble," she said, and as he did not reply, fidgeted nervously with the ribbons of her bedjacket, very conscious all at once of the alien masculine presence by her bed.

He continued to observe her, his hands in the pockets of his old slacks, and as the colour began to mount in her cheeks, he smiled suddenly, altering the whole expression of his face.

"Was I staring rudely?" he mocked gently. "It's the first time I've seen you properly—by daylight, I mean."

He came and sat on the side of the bed, and observed, as Bunny had done, how sharply defined were her bones and how light and immature she looked against the pillows.

"How do you feel?" he asked, frowning. "Northy doesn't seem very satisfied with you."

She smiled shyly.

"That's only because he thinks I'm too thin."

"You are—much too thin. You look as though you need country air and a lot of feeding."

"I've always been thin," she said apologetically. "I expect it's because I've just finished growing, but Tante says it's unbecoming. I hope she hasn't given M. Bergerac a— a false impression. The photograph she sent him a little while ago wasn't a bit like me."

"Wasn't it?"

"No. It was flattering of course, and sort of vague and smudgy in an artistic kind of way, and Marthe had dressed my hair very elaborately."

43

She was talking too much, she knew, but she was nervous, and as she saw his eyes travel to her hair, which lay soft and childishly straight on her shoulders, she put up a hand to administer an ineffectual twist to the ends.

"So you weren't inventing, after all," he said. "M. Bergerac is real and you are prepared to go through with this marriage to oblige your aunt."

"Marthe told you, I suppose."

"Oh, yes, Marthe made things very clear. Are you going to like living in France with a stranger?"

"I don't know, but Tante says that part of the Alpes Maritimes is very beautiful."

"It has it's charm, certainly."

"Is it like that?" She nodded to the photographs on the wall, and he smiled.

"Well, not quite. The Maritimes can hardly compare with the great heights of the world."

"But there are mountains?"

"Oh, yes, there are mountains. Why? Does that appeal?"

"All the time I've been up here, I've got to know those photographs," she said slowly. "I lie and think about them —Kanchenjunga . . . Everest . . . and the mountains of Switzerland—the Matterhorn, the Jungfrau, Mont Blanc and Monte Rosa—such exciting names."

He regarded her oddly, as if he was seeing her for the first time.

"You talk with nostalgia," he said. "Do you have in you this inexplicable affinity with the strange grandeur of the heights?"

"I don't know," she answered with simplicity. "No one has ever talked to me about mountains; but you—you understand all about them, don't you? You are a climber."

The eyes which had puzzled and chilled her on their first meeting were explained, she thought; they were the dispassionate, far-seeing eyes of the mountaineer. But even as she spoke she saw the change in his face.

"I'm no longer any good for that. The mountains require one's full strength, both spiritual and physical," he said, and she shrank into herself, dismayed by her stupidity. She had forgotten the handicap which slowed his movements to such deliberate stiffness.

44

"Tell me about some of your old expeditions," she said, trying a little clumsily to cover her foolishness, and wishing shyly to detain him longer, but the bitter twist was back on his lips and he replied indifferently:

"There are plenty of books on mountaineering in that bookcase, if you're interested. My own experiences don't make very enthralling hearing."

Marthe entered the room without knocking, and stood for a moment surveying them both, observing at once the flush on Sabina's cheeks and the soft distress in her eyes.

"If Monsieur had said he intended paying Mademoiselle a visit, I would have made it my business to be present," she said.

Brock rose slowly to his feet, remarking with faint mockery: "You consider a chaperone is advisable in the circumstances."

"It is not usual in my country for a stranger of the opposite sex to share the intimacies of the bedroom of a *demoiselle*," she snapped, and straightened the creased bedspread as if to remove all evidence of his presence.

"That's rude, Marthe," Sabina said with gentle dignity. "Mr. Brockman is my host, and it is perfectly usual to inquire for the health of a sick person."

"You know nothing of such matters, my cabbage—and Monsieur is not your host. He is a guest in the house of his governess, like yourself," Marthe retorted with ill-concealed malice.

"And of course," added Brock with misleading gravity, "Mademoiselle is affianced—or very nearly—which makes a difference. Your pardon, Mademoiselle Marthe—I will bid you both *au revoir*."

He had spoken in French, and Marthe's little pig-like eyes sent him a look of intense dislike, but she did not care to try any further conclusions with him, so set her lips in silence until he had left the room.

"You are unwise, mam'zelle, if you seek diversion in that quarter," she said when she heard the door close. "He would amuse himself, no doubt, at your expense, but you have not the temperament to indulge the little flutter before marriage. M. Brockman would only laugh while you imagined a *maladie du coeur* to which you are not suited."

Sabina's eyes were angry and she suddenly pounded the bed with small, clenched fists.

"You are insufferable, Marthe!" she cried. "I am no longer a child to be spoken to in this manner, neither is it your place to be insolent to another guest in this house."

Marthe folded her arms and observed the girl with an annoyance that was mixed with surprise.

"O-ho!" she observed. "So the little one makes herself airs and scratches when Madame is away. Have I not worked without wages when it suited? Have I not been loyal to Madame and guarded you from the many foolishnesses you might commit before you are safely *ranger*? Do I then deserve that you should turn upon me because I seek to observe the instructions of Madame, your aunt?"

Sabina regarded the angry woman with eyes that were grave and curiously clear.

"I am beginning to understand that neither you nor Tante cares in the least what happens to me," she said without any of her usual uncertainty. "I will oblige my aunt so long as it seems to be the right thing to do, but— don't drive me too hard, Marthe, for this bargain was not of my making, and who knows—I may not care for René Bergerac once I meet him."

"*Och*!" exclaimed Marthe, outraged. "Such talk! Such impudence! I will write to Madame this very day and acquaint her of your situation. It will not surprise me—it will not surprise me at all should she return immediately to England and remove you from these *sales* surroundings."

She spoke with venom, but she spoke, too, at random. She did not care for this fresh turn of events, nor did she consider herself capable of averting a disaster which Madame, with her stronger influence, could reduce to ridicule in a few biting phrases.

"I will write to Madame," Marthe repeated, not liking the cool regard of the young girl she had for so long dismissed as an unimportant factor in a perfectly logical arrangement. Then she slammed out of the room.

*   *   *

But it was not, in the end, Marthe who first wrote to Tante. Down in the kitchen, where Bunny was preparing

46

vegetables for the evening meal, Brock sat by the old-fashioned range, smoking a pipe and delivering himself in stronger language than Bunny cared to hear of his opinion of the Frenchwoman.

"I know," she sighed. "She can be quite intolerable. When one thinks what that poor child has probably had to put up with for years, it isn't surprising that she can view marriage with a total stranger as the lesser of two evils. The aunt must be a callous woman to care so little for the girl's happiness."

"The aunt was Lucille Faivre before she married her English husband. That might explain a lot for you," said Brock, and Bunny, the vegetable knife poised in her numbed fingers, straightened her aching back.

"Lucille Faivre . . ." she repeated slowly. "Old sins with long shadows, Brock?"

"Perhaps—or alternatively a belated twinge of conscience."

"Hardly that," said Bunny dryly. "Lucille Faivre ever looked to her own advantage, but it was before your time."

"Not altogether, but the repercussions of that affair have affected more people than those immediately concerned."

"The evil that men do lives after them," said Bunny slowly and plunged her hands again into the ice-cold water to deal with the rest of the vegetables.

"She was hardly evil, I suppose," said Brock judiciously.

"Merely a vain, selfish woman with a disregard for the normal standard of living. Strange that her niece should be so meek and sheltered as that child upstairs, but that kind are always the most conventional when it comes to their own."

"I would not like someone so inexperienced to suffer for the whims of Lucille Faivre," Bunny said; "but of course, a word from you can show her the truth about René Bergerac. There will be no need for sacrifices in any direction."

"Except Lucille Faivre," he remarked dryly. "She would scarcely remember me after all this time, but it's strange our paths should have crossed in this way."

"The mills of God . . ." she said solemnly , for she was fond of apt quotations, but he laughed a little shortly.

47

"Hardly as dramatic as that," he said. "But we might put a spoke in the wheel all the same. When does Northy say the girl can leave?"

"In a few days. She's getting up tomorrow. In point of fact, she could go any time, but Dr. Northy keeps making excuses. He has an idea that a spell of quiet rectory life would do her good."

"He may be right. What would you say to keeping her for a time—as a winter P.G.?"

Bunny tipped the dirty water down the sink, dried her hands carefully, then turned to look at him.

"What have you got at the back of your mind, Brock?" she asked with reserve. "It did not strike me that you were particularly interested in the girl when you brought her here."

"I wasn't, but you must admit the situation that has arisen is worth a glance."

"You can clear that up if you wish."

"But would it be doing anyone a kindness? Wouldn't it be better and more amusing to wean the child from her aunt's notions and make her think things out for herself?"

Bunny came and stood on the bright rag rug before the fire. Although she took the woollen mittens from the pocket of her overall and automatically pulled them over her cold hands, she gave him at the same time the straight, appraising look he remembered from boyhood.

"Are you hoping to lighten the dullness of a west-country winter for yourself?" she demanded sternly, but he only raised his eyebrows in mock disapproval.

"Really, Bunny, is that nice?" he said. "In any case, Miss Sabina Lamb is scarcely a woman, though she may be turned nineteen, and I am a hardened bachelor of thirty-five."

"You needn't boast of it so smugly," she said a little tartly. "For all your aversion to the married state, your life as far as women are concerned has not been entirely blameless."

"Possibly not, but you yourself frequently tell me that there are other ways of fulfilment than climbing mountains."

"Oh, you're hopeless when you get in this mood. You

know very well that I would never advocate casual affairs of the heart as ways of fulfilment."

"Every little helps," he said flippantly, then saw that he was beginning to distress her. "All right, my prim preceptress, I won't tease you. Will you agree to what I suggest? I know I'll have Northy's approval."

"And how will you reconcile such a proposal with Marthe and with the aunt?" she asked.

"That's very simple. You have only to write to Madame explaining as much of the circumstances as you consider advisable, and I think you'll have her agreeing to any arrangement."

"Blackmail?"

"No, the truth. I'll write myself if you like. Lucille Faivre will have every incentive to remain indefinitely at the Château Berger."

"And what of her overtures to René Bergerac?"

"They can proceed with a greater sense of security."

She tucked a stray wisp of hair neatly under the net. She was tired and she was at a loss to know what really lay at the back of Brock's mind. He had always been expert at talking in riddles.

"I don't mind about Lucille Faivre," she said wearily, "but I wouldn't like that child to get hurt. I've taken a fondness for her."

"Why should she get hurt? Her notion of René Bergerac is scarcely very romantic as it is. Don't you consider she needs time to reflect without the ever-present naggings of those two women?"

"There is still Marthe to contend with, and I don't really feel, Brock, I can put up with her much longer."

"We'll find a way to dispose of Marthe," said Brock impatiently. "Won't you give the poor little devil a chance, Bunny?"

"Well, I don't know. I must sleep on it," she said, but she knew she was wavering. Whatever doubts she had with regard to Brock's own motives, she did agree that the girl needed a respite and, in the end, might not Brock be right?

"Will you regret things when your mood changes and the child, perhaps, gets in your way?" she asked, and he smiled at her a little cryptically.

"She won't get in my way," he said. "Besides, she likes mountains."

Bunny studied his dark face, weighing matters up in her mind. She believed in fate, though she preferred to call it the intervention of the Almighty. Was it not possible that the strange crossing of their paths might mean more in the end than a disentanglement—that even for Brock some knot might be unravelled and that bitter introspection broken?

Am I a sentimental, self-deceiving old woman? she wondered impatiently, then, seeing the dark familiar lines of Brock's face already settling into indifference, she rejected her own fanciful notions.

"Very well," she said; "but if this is to be an experiment—perhaps for both of you—you must remember that the advantage is yours. Whatever the truth Sabina may discover, never let it be said that you helped her towards unhappiness."

His smile was the familiar little quirk of the mouth that he used when he detected reproof in her.

"That," he said with irritating composure, "is not my intention at all."

He knocked out his pipe on the range with a gesture of finality and took himself into the garden to gaze upon the graves.

Willie Washer, the boy who periodically worked in the garden, was pulling weeds from the base of a tombstone. He liked to work in the churchyard, although the present vicar did not approve, for Willie was simple and nobody wanted him.

Brock stood watching the ungainly figure with a rough, impatient compassion. They were two of a kind, he reflected bitterly, both incapacitated by nature for the life for which they had been intended.

"Still at it, Willie?" he said, but he spoke gently and the mild blue eyes lifted to his face with trust.

"Yes, Maister Brock," he replied with his slow, Cornish burr, "I do be terrible fond of they daid 'uns. They'm quiet-like, and I do be powerful fond of quiet."

"Yes, Willie, I know." The mountains were quiet like the dead, with the same impersonal solace. "But you won't neglect the garden, will you? Mrs. Fennell is not responsible for the churchyard any longer, you know."

The tow-coloured hair fell over the boy's rather vacant eyes.

"Mis' Fennell likes I should tend the daid," he said with simple cunning. "She likes for to see they graves neat and tidy from her window." He went on with what he was doing and took no further notice.

Poor Willie, thought Brock, moving away; he got what he wanted in the end, and Bunny would never turn him away, any more than she would turn away that little waif upstairs when she had thought things out.

* * *

The day that Sabina came downstairs was bright and sunny, and she stood at one of the windows looking out with curiosity at the expanse of moorland which lay beyond the garden. It was desolate, she thought, but there was a certain grandeur in the desolation, and even the tombstones which straggled to the edge of the lawn seemed a natural part of the wild rough country.

"You see, even the weather has changed for you," Brock said, glancing casually over her shoulder. "If you look you can see the first signs of spring—the green of the bogs, and the change in the heather before it blooms."

"Spring!" said Sabina with disbelief. "But it's the middle of winter!"

"It's nearly March, Spring sometimes comes overnight in this part of the world."

"Does it? Those hills on the horizon—are they mountains?"

"Hardly! They look like hills from this distance, but when you get close they are simply small rocky peaks, and are known as tors."

"Tor . . . what an odd word! How did they happen?"

"I don't think anyone knows. A lot of this country was volcanic, of course, which explains the contours, but Cornwall is full of strange things—old tin-workings said to date back to the Phoenicians, hide-outs going back to the smuggling days, and, of course, legends and superstitions without number. Cornish folk are a race apart."

"Is that why they think of us as foreigners?"

"Probably, though there's plenty of genuine foreign blood about here—French and Spanish. One day I'll take you to the coast and show you fishing villages which are as un-English as you can imagine."

She looked up at him, surprised by the warmth of his interest. He sounded as though he really wanted her to care for this country.

"I would have liked that," she said regretfully. "But we will have to go back to London in a day or so. I'm quite well now. Who is that boy?" She had caught sight of Willie Washer among the graves.

"That's Willie Washer," he replied. "He's supposed to help in the garden and chop wood, but he always gets back to the churchyard when he can. He loves the dead; he says they're quiet."

She shivered a little.

"How strange—and unnatural," she said. This casual acceptance of the dead at one's very door struck her as distinctly odd.

"Do you think so?"

Brock asked with amusement. "There's something to be said for poor Willie's view. He's simple, you see, and the living don't want him."

"Oh . . ." It was a little soft sound of compassion, and he watched the change in her face and the unconscious little gesture of her hands as though she would have liked to run at once to Willie and give him comfort.

"Would you like to stay for a time?" he asked abruptly, and her eyes clouded.

"Yes—yes, I think I would. I don't care much for London, and hotel life is so monotonous, but Tante would never stay in the country."

Even as she spoke she became acutely aware of him standing so close that the rough tweed of his jacket brushed her hand, and she knew with a flare of uneasy discernment that it was his own faintly alarming presence in the rectory which made her want to stay.

"Well, your aunt is away."

"Yes, but—" She began to realise that his suggestion was serious, and experienced a sharp pang of rebellion that she was not free to make plans of her own.

52

"There's no reason why you shouldn't, you know," he said. "Bunny takes a few P.G.s in the summer and is very willing to keep you here. Much less expensive than a London hotel, and better for you."

"But Marthe would never permit. She hates the country."

"Then Marthe can take a holiday elsewhere. Bunny wouldn't be sorry."

She laughed, but her reply held the disappointment of long acceptance.

"But my aunt would never give permission even if I were to write," she said. "You see, she has not met Mrs. Fennell, and I would never be allowed to stay with strangers."

She left the window and sat on a low stool by the fire, suddenly needing comfort. She liked this low, crowded room with its odd collection of bric-à-brac, its vast chimney-piece and the smoky, yellowing walls; at the moment she even liked with strange disquiet the dark, uncomfortable stranger who had caused her such confusion.

"As it happens, Bunny and your aunt *have* met—many years ago." Brock spoke from the window where he had remained and she looked up quickly.

"Mrs. Fennell knows Tante? How very queer!"

"Not really. In Bunny's old profession you run across all sorts of people. Your aunt will be quite convinced of her suitability. Bunny wrote to her yesterday."

Sabina sprang to her feet. She did not question a proposal so calmly stated, or stop to wonder how a chance acquaintance should somehow be bound up with Tante, far away in France. She was like an excited child as she ran to Brock and touched his hands with hers.

"Truly . . . truly?" she cried. "And Tante will say yes? She will allow me to remain here until—until she has concluded affairs with M. Bergerac?"

He looked down at her curiously. She was charming with life and colour in her face, he thought dispassionately, and absurd, too, with this perpetual acceptance of the omnipotence of M. Bergerac.

"I would say most certainly she will," he replied. "But for your own and everybody else's comfort in the house, I

53

would advise saying nothing to Marthe until we receive your aunt's reply."

"I've kept secrets from Marthe before," she said happily. "Mr. Brockman—it was your idea, wasn't it? You persuaded Mrs. Fennell to write?"

He drew back from her eager hands, and his face was as she remembered it first, hard and saturnine and a little forbidding.

"I?" he said with deliberate withdrawal. "It makes no difference to me; I'm only here for a little while, anyway. You have Bunny to thank, not me—and perhaps the good doctor, too."

She felt immediately chilled, and, putting her hands behind her back, edged away, feeling that it had been an impertinence to touch him.

"Yes, I see," she said. "But perhaps I would be a nuisance. Perhaps it would be better if I waited for Tante where she expects to find me."

"Bunny isn't acting from a sense of duty," he replied. "You would be doing her a good turn by bringing a little unexpected grist to the mill. Whether you turn out to be a nuisance is, of course, entirely your own affair."

It did not sound encouraging and she looked at him with her old indecision.

"I wouldn't make extra work," she said. "In fact I could help with lots of things. I only have to be shown how."

He lifted his eyebrows but made no reply, and she stood there uncertainly, not knowing what to say next.

"Well, anyway," she said at last, turning away, "you'll be able to have your room back. I'm sorry I've kept you out of it for so long."

He grinned, but still made no comment, and Sabina went slowly back to the fire and sat down to brood uncertainly on her change of fortune.

But, later, her mood altered. Even if Brock had made it clear that whether she stayed on or not made little difference to him, Bunny had been gracious.

"If you want to stay and won't be bored with our quiet life here, then I shall be very pleased, Sabina," she said. "I like you, child, and I think the break would do you good. I may seem elderly and prim to you, but a governess

54

has an odd affinity with youth. I would like to know you better, my dear."

"You are so kind, Mrs. Fennell," Sabina said humbly. "I only hope my aunt will give permission."

"I'm sure she will," Bunny replied with the same little air of certainty that Brock had shown. "And since I hope we will be friends, you had better start calling me Bunny, like everyone else."

"How did you get that name?" Sabina asked affectionately, thinking again how like a rabbit she could look at times.

Bunny smiled.

"I was a Miss Bunson in my governessing days, so the abbreviation was obvious," she said. "I remember when Brock was small we used to play an absurd game; for his surname, too, had been shortened, and we were boon companions of the wild—the rabbit and the badger."

"The badger?"

"Brock is the country name for a badger—did you not know?"

"No," said Sabina, feeling ignorant under Bunny's mild but inquiring gaze.

"There will be lots to teach you," Bunny said, looking rather pleased, and Sabina had the strange feeling that the precise, rather colourless little woman had missed her old pupils and the pleasure of imparting information to receptive minds.

But to Marthe none of them said anything. Sabina, waiting impatiently for her aunt's reply, hugged her secret to herself and paid little heed to the Frenchwoman's continual grumbling. Even the most barbed reproofs were received without resentment and Marthe began to be worried.

Sabina had shaken her confidence that afternoon when both speech and manner had been those of an adult person. Since that day her charge had been subtly different, and Marthe thought she knew where to lay the blame. This governess who had never lost the stamp of her profession and who worked in the house like one of her own servants, could have made little impression on a young girl about to marry into a rich family, but M. Brockman . . . there was the one who would turn the head of the unsophisticated with his brusque manner and his dark, disagreeable looks. If Madame could see—if Madame could only know of the risk to her plans, she would not tolerate such a situation for one moment . . .

At last Marthe brought herself to write, but before a reply could reach her Bunny had already received her own, and by the same post came, also, a letter for Sabina.

Bunny read hers composedly, conscious of the girl's eyes upon her.

"It's all right," she said at last, and passed the letter on to Brock. "Now read your own."

Sabina unfolded the pages carefully. Even after reassurance she could not believe that Tante's letter would not be full of reproaches, but it was couched in the most effusive phrases. She was enchanted, she wrote, that her dear niece should remain in the care of her old friend Mademoiselle Bunson . . . She was concerned for the health of her little one and country air was indubitably the best thing for her . . . M. Bergerac, who was taking a cure nearby, *hélas!* was in complete agreement with the arrangement . . . Sabina was to be guided by Madame until her return, which would not be immediately, for M. Bergerac had amiably extended his invitation to an indefinite date . . .

"*Well!*" said Sabina, looking quite bewildered, "Tante must have a very high regard for you, Bunny, and M. Bergerac, too. Had you met him?"

"He knows of me," Bunny replied. "Well now, Sabina, my dear, you need have no further fears. Now it is your business to grow strong and well and—and learn to play a little, too, I think."

"Play?" Sabina repeated, reflecting that such things must be long since done with. "Poor M. Bergerac," she added, "He is taking a cure. It seems to me, Bunny, that he must be rather sickly, for Tante told me long ago that he suffers from ill-health and cannot lead a full life."

"And doesn't that put you off?" asked Brock, folding the sheets of Tante's other letter and handing them back to Bunny.

"Well, I would like to know the nature of his illness," said Sabina seriously, then she caught the familiar derision in his eyes and blushed.

"Tante would not let me marry someone with a serious complaint, Mr. Brockman," she said with her nose in the air, and Bunny frowned reprovingly.

"Well spoken," she said. "And Brock, you mustn't tease. If Sabina is to be my guest for a little while, you will have to learn tolerance."

"I will retort with your own words, Bunny—well spoken!" he said with mock solemnity. "And if Sabina and I are both to be guests under your roof, she had better start calling me Brock and establish an armed truce. I don't think she likes me very much."

"Why should she?" Bunny retorted. "Your manner isn't always encouraging."

He made no attempt to put the girl at ease, but said directly:

"You don't like me very much, do you, Sabina?" She felt herself flushing as she met his ironical gaze. "Like" was a negative word when applied to such a personality and he would not care either way, she thought. She looked away to hide the confusion which must lie in her eyes, and took refuge in a childish dignity.

"I don't know you, Mr. Brockman," she answered sedately, and Bunny smiled involuntarily, while Brock himself bowed to her gravely and murmured, *"Touché . . ."*

CHAPTER FOUR

SABINA took a mischievous delight in acquainting Marthe of her aunt's decision, but she was unprepared for the torrent of abuse she received in return.

"Ha!" the woman exclaimed when she had finished reading Tante's letter to be convinced with her own eyes that Sabina was speaking the truth. "And why is there no mention of M. Brockman?"

"Why should there be?" asked Sabina with surprise. "Tante doesn't know him."

"And Madame *la gouvernante* took pains to make no mention of him herself! Do you think, mam'zelle, that if Madame, your aunt, knew of this man's presence here, and of the fashion in which you met, she would permit for one moment that you should stay? No, my cabbage, Madame would never risk the influence of a man such as he on the very eve of your betrothal to another."

Sabina grinned. Sometimes, she thought, Marthe talked exactly like a penny dreadful.

"You can make yourself easy," she said. "It makes no difference to Mr. Brockman whether I stay or go—he told me so himself. As you're always telling me, Marthe, I don't charm strange men very readily."

"As for that," Marthe retorted negligently, "it makes no matter if a man has the *ennui*—and what else would any man have staying in this house with its draughts and its graves and an imbecile boy and the so proper English *châtelaine?* You are young—you are promised to another —these things are sufficient when the hours are long and no other attractions offer."

"You're hardly very flattering," said Sabina, going a little pink.

"No, because you are a fool and do not understand men as I do. That old maid in the next room is no better, for she suffers too from girlish dreams, and because she is too old she is willing that you shall amuse him for her."

Sabina looked at the woman with profound distaste. The flat, sallow face, and the hairs on the upper lip had always had a faint repulsion for her, but never before had she

58

understood the native coarseness which was so near the surface.

"You are disgusting," she said with disdain. "I can't conceive how Tante has put up with you all these years."

"Because," said Marthe with contemptuous enjoyment, "I work for nothing when money is short, and because Madame knows well that she is not so very different herself. The veneer, oh yes, the *chic*, the grand manner when it suits, but Lucille Faivre was not so very different before she became Madame Lamb."

Sabina raised a hand as if she would strike her.

"What are you suggesting?" she demanded. "You will speak with respect of my aunt, whatever your private feelings. It is not for you to excuse your own faults by blaming an employer who has kept you in comfort for years."

"Comfort!" Marthe spat, and Sabina's eyes became cold.

"Oh, yes, Marthe, even in the cheap hotels you saw to it that you had comfort. Only I went without," she said.

The woman lowered her eyes, and when she next spoke there was more civility in her voice.

"You are growing up, mam'zelle," she said. "Or is it that already M. Brockman's influence shows? That is the way he talks—assuming the role of *grand seigneur* of which he knows nothing. And I—Marthe? Does Madame expect me to stay in this place, too?"

"She didn't mention you, as you saw for yourself. It would be better, I expect, if you returned to London."

"And expose you to a danger of which Madame knows nothing, and for which she would never forgive me? Oh, no, mam'zelle, not before I receive a reply to my own letter; for, look you, I have explained to Madame circumstances which that other one did not see fit to mention."

"You are very much afraid for your pickings, aren't you?" Sabina said, surprised by her own perspicacity.

"Pickings?"

"What you, as well as Tante, hope to make out of my marriage."

"Now, my cabbage, you are talking nonsense." Marthe was suddenly ingratiating, as Sabina had often known her be with Tante. "It is of you we think and your future—"

"And M. Bergerac of his house."

"He has a right to it, mam'zelle—you could not afford to live in one corner of it by yourself."

Sabina felt suddenly tired and her pleasure in the day's happenings was utterly quenched. It was very likely, she thought, that when Tante had read Marthe's interpretation of the situation, a telegram would follow immediately cancelling her letter.

"You must do as you think fit," she said wearily. "Until I hear differently from Tante I shall remain where I am."

"You will hear, my child—you will hear very soon," said Marthe complacently, and tucking her fat chin into her bosom settled at once by the fire for sleep.

Bunny, next door, had heard most of the conversation, and her face was white as Brock came into the room by the garden door.

"That woman is vile, obscene . . . " she told him, and recounted most of what she had overheard. "The child was admirable in her replies, but it is wrong that she should have been exposed so long to that filthy mind. Whatever Lucille Faivre's failings, she is the only relative Sabina has, and for the girl's sake should be decently whitewashed."

Brock's eyes were hard as flints.

"If the woman makes trouble for you—" he began, and she smiled a little shakily.

"Her insults don't hurt me," she said. "It's the trouble she may make for others."

"For Bergerac?" For a moment the old mockery was back.

"At the moment my concern is more for Sabina," she replied with something like the familiar reproof.

"The woman knows little of the old affair or she would have talked before," he said. "Lucille, no doubt, has taken good care to keep forgotten facts to herself. But I won't have you upset, Bunny. If the offer of your hospitality is going to rebound on yourself, then both she and the girl can go tomorrow."

"No, no," she said. "Having overheard that little exchange, I am more than ever anxious to keep the girl until—"

"Until she marries her elderly *roué?*"

60

"Until something can be resolved one way or the other," she retorted stubbornly.

Brock smiled, but he was not smiling when he woke Marthe in the next room and told her curtly that she could pack her bags.

"But monsieur, I cannot leave before Madame gives me instructions," she whined, resolving to take it out of Sabina, who, she could only suppose, had run to him with complaints.

"Then I will telegraph Madame this evening," he replied.

"*You* will telegraph?" she repeated, her small eyes narrowing.

"On Mrs. Fennell's behalf, naturally. She does not care to have you under her roof any longer in the circumstances. It is not Mademoiselle who repeated your conversation. It was overheard by Mrs. Fennell."

A dull colour stained her flat cheekbones.

"It is easy to see that you and Madame have misled Mademoiselle—and Madame Lamb, also," she said with a return to insolence.

"You will keep a civil tongue in your head," he returned sharply. "I know your kind, Marthe—grasping, loyal when it suits you for what you can get out of a bargain, but with no real consideration for anyone other than Marthe Dupont. You doubtless have your uses for Madame Lamb but you have none at all for me, or for Madame your hostess. You may stay the night since it is getting late, but you will have your things packed in readiness. The reply to my telegram will be here before morning."

The whole conversation had been conducted in French and, for the second time since meeting him, she was shocked into silence and the instinctive knowledge that for all her disparagement he was someone to be reckoned with. He did not wait for any argument, nor, clearly, did he expect it. She pulled the black wool shawl more tightly about her shoulders and shuffled upstairs to do her packing.

*   *   *

Sabina was much subdued by Marthe's uncompromising attitude. She knew nothing of Brock's intervention, but if she had it would have made little difference. It seemed only too probable that Marthe had made the most of a very nebulous situation and Tante, with the Bergerac money almost within her grasp, would take no chances.

She went out to the garden, avoiding the little grave-yard, which she was not yet used to as part of the rectory's attractions, and came upon Willie Washer tending a compost heap. He did not see her and was capering about on the graves chanting:

> *Hinty, minty cuty, corn,*
> *Apple seed and apple thorn*
> *Wire, briar, timber lock,*
> *Three geese in a flock . . .*

She drew nearer, careful to make no noise, fascinated by this new version of the singing rhymes she had known in childhood. Willie's gentle face when he thought he was unobserved had a strange aliveness, and his ungainly limbs only the awkward unco-ordination of a very young child's.

> *One flew east, and one flew west,*
> *One flew over the cuckoo's nest . . .*

He saw her and stopped suddenly, shuffling back to his compost heap with a guilty hunch of the shoulders.

"I don't know that one, Willie. Is there any more?" Sabina asked, and he grunted something unintelligible.

"There's a French counting-out rhyme I know," she said. "Would you like to hear it?" He made no reply, and she began softly:

> *Un, deux, trois, j'irai dans les bois.*
> *Quatre, cinque, six, chercher des cerises,*
> *Sept, huit, neuf, dans mon panier neuf . . .*

"It sounds funny, doesn't it?"

His attention was captured and he turned his back on the compost heap.

"Maister Brock sometimes talks like that," he said slowly.

"Yes, he speaks French, I know, though I don't think he'd bother himself much about silly rhymes."

"Silly Willie . . . Silly Willie Washer . . ." he muttered to himself suddenly, and Sabina knew he must have been taunted with that remark sometime or another.

"No, Willie, you're *not*," she said with warmth, "and you knock anyone down who says so!"

He grinned, revealing a broken tooth in an otherwise perfect mouth.

"*I* do," he said, suddenly delighted. "I goes for'm every time they says it. You'm kind, missy—like Maister Brock—" He advanced and touched her gingerly. "You'm not much more than a little maid, neither. Willie'll tell 'e some more rhymes some day or t'other."

"Thank you, Willie," she said, shy because she felt that he had made a definite concession. "I'm only afraid I may not stay very long."

"You stay, m'dear," he said with the soothing assurance of a much older person. "Old rectory don't see much life now, and me, I like the daid lying quiet over yonder."

She shivered. The strange affinity of the simple-minded boy with the dead was chilling, or perhaps the afternoon was growing cold.

"I'd like to stay," she said gently, but he had gone back to his compost heap and forgotten her, and she returned indoors.

Tante's reply came late that night. It was a long, extravagant telegram but quite clear.

Tell Marthe her letter is received and understood. She should take a holiday at once. I will communicate with her at the old address when I need her. Money will follow if required. My felicitations to my little Sabina for whom my heart is impatient until we meet again.

Marthe, who had been summoned from her room, stood at the foot of the stairs with the telegram in her hands.

"But Madame is mad!" she exclaimed, and sounded really bewildered. "She cannot know what she is doing."

"You think not?" said Brock politely.

Bunny had seen the surprise on Sabina's face at the concluding message in her aunt's telegram and his lips tightened. Lucille Faivre was playing a game which she, at least, understood very well, and she said quietly:

"Madame's instructions seem quite clear. Are you packed, Marthe? There is an early train to London in the morning. Mr. Brockman will drive you to the station."

"But I do not understand,"

"You would like a holiday, would you not? You have friends to go to?"

"Naturally—and it is not that I have any wish to remain here, you understand, Madame. I do not care for the country or the inconveniences of old houses."

"In that case," said Bunny with finality, "Madame's wishes should coincide with your own. You will be ready to leave by seven-thirty tomorrow, please."

"Mademoiselle . . ."

Sabina felt pity for the woman's bewilderment. She herself could not understand this sudden amiability on the part of her aunt. The lamplight distorted their four shadows to grotesque shapes, and, standing in the dim, cold hall of this strange house, she experienced a little stab of distrust.

"Perhaps it would be better if I went, too," she said and saw Brock's ironical gaze travel slowly to her face.

"Without seeing Penruthan?" he asked, and she averted her eyes. In the recent happenings of the past few days she had almost forgotten Penruthan.

"Don't you want to stay?" Bunny said more gently, and Sabina turned with relief from Brock's uncomfortable gaze. Bunny was familiar and kind in a forgotten nursery fashion, and she had been to a great deal of trouble to secure this little holiday for her.

"Yes, I do," she said. "It's only—well, like Marthe, I suppose I don't quite understand."

"Me, I understand very well," Marthe interposed grimly, "It is only Madame who I think has taken leave of her senses. Very well, mam'zelle, you stay, and to you and to Madame I am no longer responsible. If M. Bergerac should later ask the questions, then I am not to blame."

"M. Bergerac, we understand, is agreeable to the arrangement," Brock observed smoothly, and the French-woman uttered an exclamation of disgust and started to mount the stairs again.

Sabina watched the squat, angry figure ascending alone and tenderness suddenly flooded her face. Marthe was coarse and grasping and often not very kind, but she had been the familiar bulwark of years. Sabina ran up the stairs behind her and put an arm round the woman's shoulders.

"Marthe . . ." she said softly, but Marthe shook her off with uncaring impatience and proceeded on her way to bed.

"Well," said Brock with an impassive shrug. "It never pays to squander compassion. Now that little matter is settled, let's return to the fire."

Sabina was awake early the next morning listening for sounds of departure in the house. She heard the luggage being brought down and later Marthe's heavy footsteps passed her door but did not pause.

Was she going without saying good-bye, Sabina wondered, hurt by the thought of such indifference. She flung back the bedclothes and, shivering in the cold of early morning, reached quickly for dressing-gown and slippers. She could not let Marthe go without bidding her God-speed.

Brock and the two women were standing in the hall and they turned to watch her as she ran down the stairs, her hair flying. Bunny, who cherished memories of the pictures of her youth, thought she looked like the young Queen Victoria upon her accession as she stood at the foot of the stairs in her long robe, her eyes wide with questioning.

"Marthe!" she cried. "Were you going without saying good-bye?"

"There is no need to say anything, mam'zelle. You have made your choice," the Frenchwoman replied sullenly.

"But it's only for a short time," Sabina said. "And I, at any rate, would like to say *au revoir*."

Marthe shrugged and Brock, who already had the front door open, observed that there was no time for farewells; they would miss the train. The hall was very cold, for fires had not yet been lighted for the day, and Bunny said:

"Go back to bed, dear child. You may take cold again after the chill."

"Marthe . . ." Sabina said again, and her voice was coaxing. "You will send some clothes for me, won't you? And a little money?"

"The money is Madame your aunt's affair. I have nothing but what she chooses to send."

Sabina tried to make a joke of it.

"But we always live on your savings till Tante returns—you know we do."

"This time you must make other arrangements. Good-bye, mam'zelle," Marthe replied, and left, without adding anything more.

Bunny glanced curiously at Sabina's stricken face as Brock slammed the door behind him. It surely was not possible that the girl could have regrets for this unpleasant woman's departure.

"Marthe is not very nice, I know," Sabina said as though Bunny had spoken her thoughts aloud, "but, you see, to me she's familiar, and one misses familiar things."

"Well, I hope that my company and Brock's may compensate for that," Bunny returned a little dryly. "Personally, I do not think that any young girl should be left in the charge of such a woman."

"She's very loyal to Tante, really, and she's been our standby for years. I wish she had come to say good-bye to me, though," Sabina said.

"Well, go back to bed and I'll bring you a cup of tea," Bunny said. "This house is very chilly before the fires are lighted."

Sabina went back to her room and stood for a moment at the window, looking out on the bleak countryside. It was a grey day, and the chill of a late dawn still lay over the neglected garden and the graves beyond. It was not surprising, she thought, that Marthe had disliked the place. Sabina climbed gratefully into bed and reflected for the first time upon the comfort of constant hot water and fires that warmed at the touch of a switch.

When Bunny came up with the tea she glanced shrewdly at her guest's disconsolate face and observed:

"Have you changed your mind already about the rectory, Sabina? We live very plainly here, and there is little in the way of amusement."

Sabina coloured, feeling that she had been caught out in ingratitude.

"Oh, no," she said quickly. "It's most kind of you to

have me, and I—I expect when the sun comes out the country will look quite different."

Even as she spoke she remembered Brock telling her that other day that you could see the first hint of spring in the colours of the moor.

"I expect it wants knowing—the moor, I mean," she added.

Bunny smiled.

"Some never come to know it," she said. "The moor accepts and rejects as it chooses."

"Like Mr. Brockman," said Sabina, sipping her tea.

"Brock?" Yes, perhaps you're right. He was bred on the moor, so perhaps there's an affinity."

"But Cornwall's no longer his home, is it?"

"Not now, but Brock's had many homes in many lands. His business takes him far afield."

Sabina did not ask what Brock's business might be and Bunny did not tell her. She said instead, nodding to the photographs round the walls:

"Do you get tired of looking at them?"

"No—oh no, I love them. Sometimes I make up stories about them."

"That's fortunate, for Brock wants you to keep his room while you're here."

Sabina looked surprised and then embarrassed.

"Oh, I couldn't possibly do that," she said. "All his own things are here, aren't they? Besides, he must miss his mountains."

"Well, you must settle that between the two of you, but personally I think it mightn't be a bad thing if Brock was separated from his mountains for a time. It's no good hankering after what you can no longer have."

"Does his stiff leg mean that he can never climb again?" asked Sabina.

"Oh, yes. Climbing was finished for him some time ago —long enough for him to have learnt resignation, anyway," said Bunny.

Sabina's eyes rested with gentle thoughtfulness on a magnificent photograph of the Matterhorn.

"But do you think one ever learns that?" she asked. "I mean, for someone who has known and conquered the heights, a physical handicap must seem like an insult."

Bunny looked at her with surprise.

"How should you know that?" she said. "It is what he has tried to make me understand."

"And you cannot?"

"Not entirely. It has always seemed to me that to resent an infirmity to such a degree is an admission of failure. One should be made strong by misfortune; one should have complete freedom of spirit."

"Not at first," Sabina said. "Not until there's something else."

Bunny looked at her with humility. How did she know, this ignorant child? How should she understand with such simplicity the truth which Bunny had been trying to preach for years? But already the awareness had gone from the girl's face. She drew her knees up to her chin under the bedclothes and her expression was once more that of a shy child.

"How far is Penruthan from here?" she asked.

"Penruthan? Of course, that's really why you are here, is it not? It lies over the moor to the west."

"Is it far? Could I walk there?"

"Oh, yes, if you're not afraid of exercise, but the going can be rough. Brock should be back in half an hour for breakfast, so you had better get up now. I will put a can of hot water in the bathroom, but the bath water will not be hot, I fear, until the afternoon."

Bunny picked up the empty cup, automatically straightened Sabina's underclothes lying neatly folded on a chair, and left the room with no further speech.

*   *   *

After breakfast Sabina helped Bunny with the housework, for Mrs. Cheadle in the kitchen was suffering from her proverbial bad legs and drinking tea in vast quantities until such time when she could, with all honour, repair to her home in the village.

"I do not expect you to do this, my dear," Bunny protested once with mild reproof. "Dusting and polishing cannot be very amusing for you."

"Oh, but they are," Sabina contradicted happily.

68

"There's nothing to do like this living in hotels, and it's really terribly fascinating making things shine and scrubbing something until you *know* it's clean."

"Well, it's not the average taste," Bunny smiled. "Still, I suppose if you've never done it there's a novelty attached. Did they teach you nothing useful, your aunt and Marthe?"

"Needlework, of course," Sabina said, feeling a little guilty that she possessed so small a knowledge of domestic matters. "I do all Tante's mending and washing and I can make a *tisane* for almost any ailment, and I can market as cheaply as Marthe, though, of course, the hotels provide most of our food."

"I see." Bunny did not express any opinion as to whether she considered such things to be adequate, but she was thinking privately that Lucille Faivre had found yet another unpaid servant in her young niece.

Brock had gone out again soon after breakfast and was not expected back until the afternoon, so Sabina and Bunny had luncheon together on a small table by the fire in the living-room.

"It's an old-maidish habit, I suppose," Bunny apologised, "but so much more cosy when one is alone—and I'm alone for the most part in the winter, of course."

"I like it, too," Sabina said, enjoying the warmth of the fire on her legs and the unfamiliar intimacy of a species of indoor picnic. "Do you get lonely here, Bunny?"

"No, dear, I haven't the time," the governess replied. "When my husband was alive, of course, it was rather different, but although I no longer have much to do with the parish, the new vicar's wife up on the hill is always glad of a little help."

Sabina could not picture Bunny with a husband. It was easier, by far, to think of Marthe as a married woman.

"What was he like—Mr. Fennell, I mean?" she asked shyly, and Bunny smiled.

"You are wondering how I came to be married at all, are you not?" she said. "My husband was a widower. I came here as governess to his little boy who died not long after. He married me because—well, probably because he was lonely, and this is a big house for a man alone."

69

Sabina was silent. It was rather a joyless little history, she thought, and understood how much Brock's infrequent visits probably meant to his old governess.

"He was your favourite?" she asked, and Bunny gave her an amused look.

"You mean Brock? Yes, perhaps he was. He had a difficult childhood in many ways. His parents were separated, and that's always sad for a child."

"Sadder than having none?"

"Well, that would depend, I suppose. Do you not remember your own parents, Sabina?"

"My mother died soon after I was born and my father didn't want to be bothered with a child, I think," Sabina said. "Even then I used to go on visits to Tante. She hadn't long been married to my uncle, and I remember we all thought her very gay and smart."

"And she was willing to act as your guardian?"

"There was no one else. My uncle died the same year as my father and neither of them left much money. Tante has often said that if it hadn't been for me she would undoubtedly have married again."

"Indeed? But Penruthan, no doubt, seemed a safer proposition."

"Penruthan?"

Bunny pursed her lips and looked embarrassed.

"Forgive me, my dear, I should not have said that," she said, "but both you and Marthe have been a little free with your affairs."

"Have we?" asked Sabina, who had never imagined that the reason for Tante's adopting her had not been known to everyone. "Well, of course, if it had not been for Penruthan, I don't suppose Tante would have been so hasty, but it was not unreasonable to suppose that by selling it we could both be more comfortably off, was it?"

"It was a pity, in that case, that the legal side of the matter was not gone into first," remarked Bunny dryly, but Sabina only smiled at her.

"Yes; but, you see, Tante didn't know much about English law then, and I, a schoolgirl, didn't even know I had inherited a house."

"I see," said Bunny, and said no more. Indeed it was

only too plain that the child Sabina had been used with scant regard for her own well-being.

It was Bunny's afternoon for the Women's Institute, so Sabina would be left by herself until Brock returned.

"I shall go out," she said, and thought of Penruthan over the moor.

"Yes, dear, explore the garden," Bunny said absently; "but wrap up warmly; there's no sun today."

Left alone in the big house, Sabina experienced that strange delight that follows the unexpected possession of someone else's property. She ran from room to room, making herself familiar with hitherto unnoticed objects, examining books and pictures, picking up ornaments, and lingering longest over the framed snapshots of children, the only family Bunny had ever known. There were some quite recognisable as Brock at various ages, from sailor suit to the first rough tweeds of adolescence. Where were they now, Sabina wondered, these old-fashioned children with their dated clothes? Did any of them return as Brock did to keep faith with their childhood days, or had they forgotten?

She sighed and went upstairs to put on her coat and strong shoes. This was a house built for children, she thought, listening to the empty echoes of her own footsteps on the stairs. There were a few forgotten toys put away in cupboards and old books much scribbled over, with fascinating pictures of boys and girls in old-fashioned clothes and little dogs with lolling tongues and eyes like saucers. In the days of large families, the rectory children would have raced through the house, shouting and calling, and played among the tombstones, never remembering that the dead lay there. What had Brock said? *Very salutary to live close to the dead. . .* It was the kind of remark one would expect of him, she thought and laughed, dispelling the faint melancholy which had fallen upon her for no known reason.

It was very cold outside, and the sky was leaden, with no break in the grey expanse which met the moor's horizon. "Cold enough for snow," Bunny had observed this morning, and even as Sabina climbed the low wall of loose stones which marked the western boundary, the first flakes fell softly on her face and hair. It was as well she

71

had chosen today to visit Penruthan, she thought, for if snow came, the tracks across the moor would be hidden and she would not find the way.

Willie Washer's tow-coloured head appeared suddenly from amongst the graves.

"Where be to?" he asked. He had accepted her presence at the rectory with caution, but he seemed to acknowledge her now as a not so different counterpart of himself.

"I'm going to find Penruthan," she said, poised on top of the wall. "Would you come with me a little way, to show me the path?"

"Penruthan?" he said and shook his head. "Nay, 'tes 'aunted. Leave me be with me graves."

"Not a little way, Willie?" she said, but he turned his back on her.

"Nay, not me. You'm proper mazed, missy. Snow's a-coming."

She tried to coax him a little more, but he had sunk into one of his silences and would not respond.

Soon she began to realise that west over the moor was not as simple as it sounded. The rough tracks crossed and recrossed and sometimes petered out altogether, and presently she abandoned them and struck out across heather and boulder, following her nose as best she might. Bunny had said the moor was rough going; one was evidently not meant to follow a path.

When she had walked for an hour or more, Sabina knew that she was lost. It was snowing fast now, and already the countryside was covered with a thin film of white. Behind her all trace of the rectory and the little village beyond had long since vanished from sight, and as far as the eye could see the moor stretched endlessly on every side. She began to grow afraid. She had no notion of how far this rough country extended, and she remembered Brock's tales of the ancient mines and workings, pitfalls for the unwary; dark places in which to break a limb or be lost for ever from sight.

Her muscles were aching painfully from the unaccustomed exercise and snow blinded her continually, causing her to stumble and fall. But she must go on. Somewhere, sometime, there must be a road; better to go forward and meet what might come than try to retrace her steps in the gathering dusk.

As she plodded wearily on she thought of Marthe, safe now in the heart of London, and of Tante in her brightly lit hotel, even now, perhaps, drinking an *apéritif* with M. Bergerac, happily returned from taking his cure, and at the thought of the unknown M. Bergerac, in her imagination so like the sleek *maîtres d'hotel* of her acquaintance, Sabina found herself laughing out loud.

It was quite dark now. She put out both hands instinctively as the blackness ahead looked suddenly impenetrable, and touched the cold solidity of stone. It was a wall, she thought with surprise, as looking up, she saw the paler darkness of the sky beyond. She must be a little light-headed, she decided, for walls do not rise suddenly out of moorland. A faint creaking sound caused her heart to beat faster, but as she moved towards it and came upon an opening, she knew that it must be a door in the wall, left open and creaking a little in the wind that was getting up. She remembered the hidden door in *The Secret Garden*, that cherished book of her childhood, and stepped carefully through the opening, knowing that nothing which lay the other side could surprise her.

At first she could make out little in the darkness. She only knew that the character of the ground had changed, that under the snow lay turf and the slippery smoothness of flagged paths. The ground seemed to rise in terraces and there were broken steps, and a stone balustrade under her hand. As she mounted the last steps her feet crunched on gravel and she saw a house, vast and shuttered, stretching, it seemed, endlessly into the darkness.

"Penruthan . . ." she murmured and touched the wet cold walls with undoubting certainty. Had she not walked west as she was told, and had not instinct led her home? It was only then that she knew how tired she was, how much her legs ached and how numb with cold were her hands, indeed, her whole body. She sank down gratefully in the snow and, leaning against the wall of the house, thought blissfully of sleep. She must have dozed while the snow piled in a little drift in her lap, for something woke her. She listened; then as she was about to slip once more into sleep she heard it again; a man's voice shouting.

She thought it was her own name that was called, but the mountains played tricks, she remembered, and if you started imagining things you went mad . . .

The shouting came again, much nearer, and this time she knew that it was her name that was called. At the same moment she saw the light of a torch mark somebody's passage round the end of the house, and she replied at once. It was Brock, of course. She could see his stiff, dragging walk in the light of his torch and the strange shadows of buttresses and pillars sprang out from the house as he passed.

"Where are you?" he called.

"Here," she replied, making no attempt to rise, and presently he was standing over her and flashing the beam of his torch upon her. She blinked up at him in the light but said nothing.

"Are you hurt?" he asked sharply, and when she shook her head, ordered her to get up at once.

She obeyed, conscious of acute pins and needles in her legs.

"I heard you shouting," she said.

"Then why the hell didn't you answer at once?"

"I thought it was the mountains. The books say that if you're lost the mountains play tricks."

"You're not in the mountains, you crazy little idiot. Did you think a bit of snow gave you an excuse to play games with yourself and everyone else?"

"You're angry," she said with surprise, and he took her by the shoulders and shook her.

"Of course I'm angry," he retorted. "What possessed you to run away again without a word to Bunny?"

"I didn't run away. I came to find Penruthan. This is Penruthan, isn't it?"

"Yes. How did you get here?"

"I came across the moor—going west."

The light threw strange shadows on his face. He wore no hat and snow had settled on his hair, giving him the look of an older, kindlier man.

"Brock . . ." she said, using his nickname for the first time. "Don't be angry . . . I had to find Penruthan by myself, didn't I?"

74

She rested her head on his breast, because she was too tired to remember that they were strangers, and for a moment he held her there, recognising a spirit that had once been his own, then he pushed her away with an impatient gesture.

"You might have known that Bunny would have been alarmed," he said. "Really, Sabina, you haven't much consideration for your hostess, have you?"

"I'm sorry," she said, humbly. "But she said Penruthan lay west over the moor, and I didn't think I would get lost."

"I don't suppose she imagined that a town-bred girl would venture on the moor without a little more knowledge," he retorted. "Do you know west from south or north from east?"

"Yes, I think I do."

"Well, that's debatable. I think luck brought you here—and, possibly, an endurance that we neither of us had suspected. Would you have stayed here all night?"

"I suppose I would. I was so tired, you see, and after the moor it seemed shelter. How did you know where to look?"

"We didn't until Willie came out with some garbled story," he said with grim rebuff; "but Penruthan seemed worth a visit. Now, if you've had enough of your adventure, we'd better be getting home. Bunny is worried."

He turned to retrace his steps along the terrace without waiting to see if she followed, and at her first attempt to walk the cramps in her legs almost made her fall.

"Wait . . ." she cried, "I've the most terrible pins and needles . . . I can't move."

He turned and flashed his torch on her again, but his voice was hard and unsympathetic as he replied:

"That's not surprising. Exercise will get the circulation back. Come along—I'm not prepared to carry you."

She moved towards him and the pain in her legs made her cry out. He put an impatient hand under her elbow and together they walked slowly to the front of the house, where his car was standing.

He had left his headlights on, and in the twin beams Sabina could see the outlines of the great house, the porch

75

with its studded door, the stone supports of mullioned windows reaching high above her.

"It's so big," she said. "How queer to think I should own it."

"Not the best moment to have chosen to inspect your property," Brock observed dryly, opening the door of his car.

"Oh, yes, it is," she said, gazing at the house with eyes that were hypnotised by the snow and the sudden light, "It will never again seem quite the same, will it?"

"Get in," he replied, unfeelingly, and, when she still stood there as if he had not spoken, he picked her up in a grip that was none too gentle and pushed her into the car.

Tears came as he turned down a short drive and out on to the snowy road, tears of exhaustion and the emotional reaction to a new and strange experience.

"You cry very easily," he remarked, and she expostulated with the indignant shame of a child;

"I don't. But I'm not used to days like this—being lost in a blizzard and discovering an inheritance at the same time."

She thought he smiled in the darkness, but the snow could play tricks as well as the mountains and she was not sure.

"Hardly a blizzard," he said, "though it may be one before morning. You are not at all fitted for the future your aunt has planned for you, Miss Sabina Lamb."

"Why?"

"Because you will expect miracles—or, at least, romantic manifestations—and a marriage of convenience is not likely to provide either."

"Oh," she said a little blankly, then, aware suddenly that she had received little consideration from him, she added severely:

"I don't think you've been very kind, Mr. Brockman. I haven't been attempting a difficult mountain, I know, but the experience was quite gruelling enough for a first attempt."

"Yes, for a first attempt I think it was," he replied with unexpected agreement, "but don't let it give you exalted ideas. Your path is set in ordered places. Initiative is not for you."

"I might have got another chill," she said, trying to assert her own importance.

"If you have," he returned, unimpressed, "you will be tiresome rather than interesting. Bunny's P.G.s are not expected to give trouble."

She was silent after that, and it was not long before they reached the rectory. Bunny herself was standing at the open door while the snow drifted gently over the threshold.

"Thank God!" Bunny said fervently, and her face looked old and pinched. "Did you find her at Penruthan, Brock?"

"Yes. She'd taken a bee-line straight across the moor. She seems to think that was quite an achievement."

Over Sabina's head, Bunny met his quizzical look with raised eyebrows.

"I think it was," she replied quietly, and as Sabina began to cry, she led her away into the warmth of the living-room.

CHAPTER FIVE

WHEN Sabina awoke the next morning the character of her room had subtly altered. A hard snowlight touched the white walls with cold brilliance and the mountains in the photographs stood out, clear and defined. Sabina ran to the window to look out on the changed countryside and caught her breath at the sudden beauty of the landscape. The bleak savagery of the moor was hidden by the unbroken expanse of snow, and blue shadows gave the hollows the semblance of glaciers to her enchanted eyes. The tors on the horizon looked like distant mountains with their covering of snow, and even the graves beyond the garden had taken kindlier shapes.

Sabina dressed with feverish haste, not wanting to miss a moment of such delight, and she reached the little back parlour where they breakfasted before Bunny had made the coffee.

"You were meant to breakfast in bed," Bunny said, sounding quite flustered. "I trust you have not taken another chill after your experience yesterday. You should have waited until I called you, dear."

Brock, glancing up from his morning's mail, observed dryly:

"You sound like the proverbial hen with one chick. Such concern!"

"Well, it's more han *you* showed me," Sabina retorted somewhat tartly, and he grinned.

"Quite right," he said. "I'm glad to see you can answer back."

He did not sound concerned one way or the other, neither did he ask her how she was, and she gave him a look of dislike and sat down at the table.

Bunny brought the coffee and poured it out, remarking that it was a day to remain indoors and keep warm, but Sabina, her eyes on the frosted windows, said:

"But I don't want to miss a moment of it! I want to go out in the snow as soon as I've had my breakfast."

"No further than the garden, then," warned Bunny, and Brock, with faint irony, inquired:

"Haven't you ever seen snow before?"

"No" Sabina replied simply. "In London the snow never stays, but here the country is transformed. Is it anything like—like Switzerland?"

"Switzerland?" repeated Bunny, puzzled.

"She means the mountains," Brock said with a quirk of the eyebrows. "She has an obsession about them—why, I can't think. Perhaps my photographs get into her dreams."

"Perhaps they do," said Sabina, giving him a strange look. "You are rather like the mountains yourself—cold and craggy and impersonal."

"Dear me!" said Brock mildly. "Do I get into your dreams, too?"

But she flushed faintly and paid close attention to her breakfast, so did not see Bunny's raised eyebrows or the glance of reproof she bestowed upon Brock.

"You are both talking a great deal of nonsense," Bunny said. "There's more snow to come down, so you must get out of doors early, Sabina. You are sure you have no chill?"

"I feel wonderful," Sabina replied happily, and, indeed, in her thick scarlet sweater, with the light hair tumbling carelessly over her forehead she had a fleeting radiance. She had accepted them, Bunny thought curiously; even Brock with his sharp tongue and his apparent unconcern for finer feelings. Perhaps with the temporary severing of old ties she had come into her own.

"Then enjoy yourself in your own fashion," Bunny said and unaccountably sighed.

Willie was sweeping snow from the little back yard, and Sabina tried to get him to throw snowballs with her, but it was one of his sullen days. He looked angry when a handful of snow hit him, and raised his shovel threateningly.

"Willie!" warned Bunny's voice from the kitchen window, and he shuffled off to the other side of the yard and took no further notice of Sabina.

"Poor Willie," Bunny said, "the children used to throw stones at him, you know, and sing a horrid rhyme they made up about him to make him angry. He doesn't understand snowballing."

Sabina walked round the house, her heart quick with compassion. In his way Willie Washer had grown up much as she had herself, she supposed, for he, too, had never learnt to play.

She spent a happy morning in the garden, kicking up the snow with childish delight, and even balancing on the shrouded tombstones as if they meant no more than the familiar landmarks of every day.

"How disrespectful!" said Brock's voice behind her, and she turned to find that he was standing on the snowy lawn, watching her.

"Is it?" she asked anxiously. "Do you think the dead would mind?"

"Very unlikely, I should think," he replied. "They've most of them lain there for as long as you've been alive or longer. Tell me, Sabina, did you never learn to play like this when you were a child?"

"No," she said, and thought of Willie. "There was no one to play with. Oh, look! A robin—and I think it's hurt."

She stooped and gently picked up the bird at her feet. It hardly struggled, but its eyes were fixed and bright with alarm.

"Let me see," said Brock, opening her fingers with a touch that was curiously gentle. "It's damaged its wing, I'm afraid. Probably flew into one of the tombstones. Make a little hollow for it in the shelter of this grass."

"But it will die if we leave it here in the cold with no food," she said, and raised suddenly anguished eyes to his.

He knew a strange moment of repudiation as he watched her, the bird held against her breast, as if the pity which flowed from her were a tangible thing to hold and swamp him.

"Then bring it into the kitchen if you must," he replied impatiently. "Bunny will, doubtless, support your sentiments, though the bird is sure to die."

She carried the robin carefully indoors, aware that Brock did not follow her, and made a nest in an old work-basket of Bunny's and set it by the fire. Mrs. Cheadle had already gone and Bunny was preparing soup for Willie's lunch.

"Brock says it's sure to die, but it won't, will it, Bunny?" she pleaded.

"Not if we can help it," Bunny assured her briskly. "Wild birds don't take kindly to captivity, but robins are tamer and more trusting than most. We will give it some warm milk with a drop of brandy."

"Why does he like to seem unkind—Brock, I mean?" Sabina asked. "He looked at me as if—as if he resented me being sorry for the robin."

"Brock's afraid of pity, even if it's indirect," Bunny said composedly, "but he's many times brought maimed creatures into the warm when he was a boy, and cured them, too."

He came into the kitchen as she spoke, knocking the snow from his shoes.

"Well, you're more likely to choke the little perisher if you feed it like that. Here—let me do it," he said, and taking the spoon from Bunny, knelt down on the hearth beside them.

Sabina sat back on her heels, observing the delicacy with which he handled the bird and the expert care with which he coaxed a few drops of liquid down its throat. His hands were strong and shapely, she noticed with surprise, and his dark face, intent on his work, had an unconscious tenderness.

Bunny had gone out to the woodshed with Willie's soup, and Brock looked up suddenly, aware of the girl's silent gaze.

"Why are you staring at me with those wide, puzzled eyes?" he demanded mockingly. "Are you afraid I'll wring the creature's neck if you turn your back?"

But his sharpness did not disconcert her now. She only shook her head slowly and said:

"What a strange man you are! I don't believe you ever think before you speak."

His eyebrows rose in the forbidding, saturnine twist.

"Perhaps I think too much," he replied cryptically; "but that can't be applied to you, can it? You confide in perfect strangers and have few reticences."

"Oh, yes, I have," she answered gravely. "One is taught reticence by other people, I think. Until I came here I had learnt to hold my tongue in a different way. I'm sorry if my confidences have embarrassed you, Mr. Brockman. I have only tried to explain my actions."

"For heaven's sake, you're talking just like Bunny! Why should you embarrass me?" he exclaimed with irritation.

"And if you start calling me Mr. Brockman I shall address you as Miss Lamb. You have a curious kind of wisdom in you, haven't you?"

She looked really startled.

"I? Oh, no. Tante has always told me I'm foolish and ignorant, and Tante is usually right."

"It's not the kind of wisdom your aunt would recognise or understand," he said dryly, laying the robin back in the basket. "You have an exploring mind, Sabina—are you really content to let it lie fallow with a husband who has been chosen for you?"

For once he spoke without his usual irony, and Sabina knew a sudden brief desolation of spirit.

"I've never been encouraged to have an independent opinion," she replied a little bleakly, "and Tante expects me to marry."

"Very properly, but René Bergerac isn't the only man in the world."

"He's the only man that Tante will agree to," she said with unexpected mischief. "Besides, you've forgotten Penruthan."

"Ah, yes, Penruthan . . ." he said with becoming gravity. "You feel, I think you said, that the Bergeracs are more entitled to Penruthan than you are."

"Well, yes, I do. I don't feel Madame Bergerac had the right to leave it away from her family just for spite."

"For spite?"

"It can't have been anything else, can it? She never knew me."

"No doubt what Bergerac thinks himself. He sided with his father by all accounts."

"Yes. I don't think his mother can have been a very nice woman, even though—even though—"

"Even though Bergerac senior was not altogether faithful? Wouldn't you mind, then, if your husband sometimes looked in other directions?"

She missed the familiar note in his voice and replied quite seriously:

"I don't know much about such things; but it's the French way, isn't it?"

He got to his feet, suddenly pulling her up beside him.

"Yes, it's often the French way, and the British and every other nation under the sun, if it comes to that; but it's not usual to go into marriage expecting the worst."

He made her a little nervous, standing over her and voicing the very thoughts which had sometimes troubled her.

"But you see," she said, trying carefully to explain her unnatural feelings, "when it's not a question of love one hasn't the same right to—well, to perfection. Tante has explained that a wise woman can be happier if she recognises from the start that marriage is a business contract."

His face was grimly decisive as he searched for the truth in hers.

"You've learnt your lesson well, my obliging little innocent," he said. Well, let's hope you won't wake up one fine morning to find that platitudes can be misleading as well as untrue."

"Did you?" she asked shrewdly, and his eyes were suddenly frosty and impersonal.

"I've discovered many unpleasant fallacies in my time, but I don't think I've ever tried to live by platitudes," he said. "You'd better give it a little mature thought. I wouldn't like you to end up a disillusioned woman."

"Why should you care?" she asked, feeling she was getting the worst of the discussion.

"True, why should I?" he agreed with his usual unconcern, and she experienced a most unfamiliar desire to hit him.

*   *   *

It began to snow heavily by the afternoon, and Bunny said that they had better be resigned to the house for the rest of the day. Brock, however, went out to chop wood, despite the weather, for Willie had gone home, and the elderly woman and the young girl glanced at each other across the firelit hearth with that sense of companionship women can share when a masculine presence is removed for a time.

"I'm glad to have you here, Sabina," Bunny said. "I feel I've known you for a long time."

"Me too," said Sabina ungrammatically, and Bunny automatically smiled reproof. "But I hope I'm not spoiling Mr. Brockman's visit. He doesn't seem to be the sort of man who would enjoy purely feminine society for long."

Bunny was darning linen and she smiled as she bent over her work.

"Do you think so? Brock has had plenty of feminine friends. He has an eye for an elegant woman, you know."

"Has he?" Sabina sounded surprised and immediately imagined a succession of anonymous lovelies, chic and witty like Tante, who would know how to answer those uneasy ironies.

"That surprises you?" Bunny asked. "Women find him attractive, you know."

Sabina remained silent, and, looking up, Bunny observed the faint colour in her cheeks.

"That, I can see, is more understandable to you," she said primly and watched the blush deepen. "I believe many women like that rather hard casualness in a man."

"Is it only a pose, then?"

"Oh, no, it's not a pose. Brock's heart still lies with his mountains, I fear. That's why he's never taken a wife."

"It would be difficult," Sabina said slowly, "to live with someone in isolation on a mountain top."

"No more difficult than living with a man one had never seen," said Bunny mildly, and Sabina held out her hands for the linen in the governess's lap.

"Let me do it," she said quickly. "You'll strain your eyes in this light."

Bunny handed over the work without protest and let her pince-nez swing idly by their thin gold chain.

"That's very good of you, dear," she said. "Fine work has become rather trying for me now, and I was never a very good needlewoman, alas."

They were sitting silently, one on each side of the cavernous fireplace, when Brock returned from his labours, and he flung himself into a chair between them and lazily watched Sabina at work.

"What a domestic scene," he observed. "I didn't think any young woman plied her needle these days—but of course you had a French upbringing, Sabina."

She thought she detected the old derision in this remark, and remembering Bunny's mild rebuke earlier, replied sedately:

"I like sewing. When one's hands are occupied it's easier to arrive at conclusions."

"A profound observation," he said with amusement. "But you haven't had time, yet, to reach many conclusions, have you?"

"Now, Brock . . ." murmured Bunny, but Sabina answered gently:

"No—but isn't that why I'm here?"

He frowned and said impatiently:

"Don't pay any attention to me. You're so young and absurd that I can't resist trying to get a rise. It looks as if this weather has set in, Bunny. Have you enough supplies in case the roads become impassable?"

"I think so. Oil is the only thing we might run short of," Bunny replied. "Perhaps you had better fetch some more from the village tomorrow."

"Will we be snowed up?" asked Sabina, raising a flushed, expectant face from her work.

"I shouldn't think so," Brock answered, then smiled with unexpected gentleness. "It's all a great adventure, isn't it, Sabina? You'll be really disappointed if we aren't besieged here?"

Her mouth curved into shy tenderness.

"It is an adventure for me," she said, "But I wouldn't like Bunny to be inconvenienced by the snow, of course."

"Snow . . . mountaains . . . I wonder why they hold such enchantment for you?" he said with the same strange gentleness.

"I don't know," she replied, her eyes wide and clear. "Perhaps those who can never experience achievements in high and snowy places can still share the magic—even if it's only imagined."

A log shifted on the open hearth, sending up a shower

of sparks, and the peat which supported it crumbled into ash, filling the room with an aromatic scent.

"Yes . . ." said Brock reflectively. "Yes . . ."

Bunny cleared her throat and remarked that it was getting too dark for Sabina to see what she was doing, but even when the lamp was lighted and the curtains drawn against the snowfilled twilight, Brock's mood lingered. He seemed fascinated by watching Sabina work. Her face bent over the snowy linen was charming in its unawareness. The soft hair fell forward in smooth sobriety over the sharp planes of her cheekbones, and the crescent curves of her downcast lids were full and tender in the firelight. He became a little hypnotised by the needle which flashed in and out under her fingers with the most delicate care.

His mood was unchanged when tea was brought, and he laughed at the butter running down Sabina's chin as she ate crumpets with frank enjoyment and, afterwards, he fetched his books on mountaineering and spread maps on the floor to illustrate a climb.

He was very like a small boy displaying his treasures, Bunny thought, watching them, and as Sabina's absorbed face caught her eyes, she gave a little sigh and removed the tea-things unnoticed by either of them.

To Sabina it was like entering a new world as he explained the technical terms of mountaineering to her. She was quick, he found, to grasp the significance of detours and weather conditions, and listened with rapt attention to his stories of the strange phenomena to be found in the mountains.

"You have the makings of a climber, I think," he said, her enthusiasm taking him back to his own early days.

"No, no," she said quickly. "I wouldn't have the courage. To climb in the greatest sense must mean, I think, complete singleness of purpose."

"I would have said you had that—or the makings of it."

"Not as you have. Perhaps it's different for a woman—perhaps one's sex is hampering. A woman would demand more of life, I think, than climbing mountains."

She was still lying flat on her stomach on the floor, her elbows propped on the spread sheets of a map. He regarded her delicate face with a preoccupied air.

"You think, like Bunny, that mountaineering is not a complete form of fulfilment?" he asked.

"Does Bunny think that? But she is a woman. A man, I think, can more easily isolate things. You Brock, have had only one love, haven't you?"

"Why do you talk with such assurance—you who have not known love at all?"

"I have no assurance, really, only—"

"Only what?"

"Somehow, one knows these things. It's like knowing one's own limitations, I suppose."

The gaze he suddenly bent on her was dark and brooding.

"Yet you are prepared to embark on one of the great adventures of life with no more perception than a school-girl," he said.

Her eyes strayed from the map and searched his face uneasily.

"It's different for me," she said. "I've grown up in a tradition, and perhaps I'm not born for great experience."

"You're born with the gift for talking a great deal of rubbish," he said crossly. "Really, Sabina, I hardly know which I'm speaking to, sometimes—a child of unusual perception or an adolescent nitwit."

"There's no need to be rude," Sabina said, and he laughed.

"Well, it's sixteen years since I was your age," he said. "I expect I've forgotten how confused one can be at nineteen."

"Brock—Bunny said you wanted me to keep your room while I'm here, but I think you should have it back."

"Do you? Why?"

"Because—well, because it's stamped with your personality—the books and the pictures and things."

He smiled a little crookedly.

"Well, live among the mountains for a little longer. I have them within me," he said. "Have you fed your robin again?"

"Oh, no, I'd forgotten!" she cried, immediately diverted, and she scrambled to her feet, pushing the hair from her eyes. "Brock—when can I see Penruthan again—properly, I mean?"

"Tomorrow, if you like," he answered carelessly. "But this time you'll come with me in the car."

"Thank you," she said and hesitated, and he remarked with his old indifference:

"I can wait outside if you want to go over it alone, but there's nothing much to see. Only a few of the rooms are furnished."

She fingered the handsome *armoire* which had first caught her attention in the crowded room.

"Is it French?" she asked, because, for some reason, she wanted to linger.

"Yes. It's said to be by Boulle, if your French upbringing has included any mention of him."

She shook her head, and he said with faint irony: "You should study the masters, Sabina. You will find furniture like that at the Château Berger. You mustn't show your ignorance to René Bergerac."

"Will he expect knowledge of such things?" she asked a little anxiously.

"Undoubtedly—unless he is the type of man who prefers to do his own educating, which I think he might be. Don't look so alarmed. Haven't you been told that reformed rakes make the best husbands?"

"Y-yes. Is a rake the same as a *roué*?"

"It's a matter of opinion, I should say. You'll find out in due course. Now what about this starving robin?"

He was laughing at her again, but he also wanted to get rid of her, she thought. An hour of her solitary company was, doubtless, as much as he could manage without becoming disagreeable.

She went out to the kitchen, where she found Bunny cleaning silver, and started to heat some milk on the stove.

"Has Brock converted you to climbing?" Bunny asked, not interrupting her task of polishing.

"He's a different person when he talks about mountains, isn't he?" Sabina said, but she did not sound very sure of the outcome of the conversation.

"Well, that applies to us all when we can mount our hobby-horse, doesn't it?"

"I suppose so, only—"

"Yes?"

"I—I wish he wouldn't sneer at M. Bergerac."

"Perhaps," suggested Bunny, "he hasn't a very high opinion of M. Bergerac."

"Oh!" said Sabina, discovering with surprise that Brock's good opinion of the man she was to marry should matter.

She took the warm milk off the stove and sat down on the floor to feed the robin in silence.

*   *   *

It had stopped snowing by nightfall, and in the morning the sun would shine from a cloudless sky to lend a sparkling beauty to the white landscape, but it was still dark when Sabina ran downstairs in her dressing-gown to heat milk for the robin.

The house was bitterly cold and icicles clung to every window, but the kitchen still retained its warmth; the range must have been replenished. Copper and brass reflected a glow from the fire and a rosy pattern danced on the flags. It was a nice kitchen, Sabina thought, aware for perhaps the first time of the reality of a home that was not a hotel. When she had fed her bird she would make tea and take it up to Bunny as a surprise.

But the robin was dead. She found it cold and stiff in the workbasket, its beak a little open, and its claws stretched in mute defeat to the ceiling.

Sabina knelt on the bright rag rug and looked at the bird with a sorrow that was touched with bitter self-reproach. She had left it there to die and never thought to feed it through the night. She lifted it from the basket and held it between her breasts, trying vainly to warm it back to life, and her tears fell gently on the soft red feathers.

Someone came into the kitchen and she raised her face to Brock. He was unshaven and probably shirtless, for he had knotted a handkerchief round his throat and tucked the ends carelessly into his coat.

"It's dead," she said tragically; "I let it die."

He knelt down beside her and took the robin from her cold hands, but she tried to snatch it back.

"If I warm it . . ." she began, but he laid the little body back in the basket and closed the lid.

"My dear child, it's quite stiff," he said with faint impatience. "It must have been dead an hour or more. I told you yesterday that this would probably happen."

"I let it die," she said again. "If I'd sat up—or come down during the night to feed it—it might have lived."

The early light of day was beginning to filter through the windows, and his face looked hard and discouraging in the greyness.

"It would have made no difference, if that's any comfort to you," he said. "I fed it several times through the night and kept the fire up. I saw it wasn't going to live."

Her tears fell faster. She had a forlorn desire to rest her head against his breast and find comfort.

"Oh, Brock . . ." she said, "Bunny told me how you used to bring maimed creatures into the warm and tend them when you were a boy. You are so much kinder than you want people to think, aren't you?"

"Do you think so?" he said a little caustically. "You're like most women—confuse kindness with sentimentality. For heaven's sake! Why do you have to weep over such a trivial commonplace? The bird would have died in any case."

His voice was still impatient, but his fingers as he brushed away her tears were curiously gentle, and when he next spoke, his voice was gentle, too.

"This is a personal loss for you, isn't it?"

"Yes," she said, and no longer minded his impatience. "It was the first live thing that I have ever had—the first creature for which I've been responsible."

"Yes, I see," he said and he smiled with sudden tenderness. "You are one of the ones who will be hurt by life, you know. You should think of that when you contemplate marriage with a stranger."

She blinked at him uncertainly, and for the first time René Bergerac, from being a nebulous, unreal character, became more sharply defined, a man whose desires were already spent and who did not really want her.

"I'm sorry," she said stiffly. "I'm not usually emotional."

"Aren't you? Well, perhaps half-past six in the morning is a little early. We'd better make some tea."

He got to his feet and began to set out cups and saucers on a tray with the ease of long practice. She watched him fill a kettle and spoon tea into an old brown teapot, and the small domestic ritual made him seem friendly and familiar. Just so, she used to imagine, would a husband and wife share the small trivialities of marriage, a sharing which might not be for her. M. Bergerac, she felt sure, would never penetrate to his own well-staffed kitchens, or pour tea carelessly into cups which did not match the saucers.

She sighed as Brock handed her one and he observed with unflattering raillery that her nose was pink and she had better swallow her tea as hot as possible.

"Crying is apt to make one's nose pink," she retorted with spirit. "And you aren't looking your best yourself, if it comes to that. Your chin is blue."

He laughed and ran a hand over his face.

"Quite right—I need a shave," he said. "What an odd mixture you are, Sabina Lamb."

"I think you're an odd mixture yourself," she replied. "I never quite know where I am."

"Don't you? Ah, well, you haven't much experience as yet. Do you still dislike me, I wonder, or will you put me in my place again by saying you don't know me?"

"It can make no difference to you which I say. I don't think you mind what people think of you."

He sat on the edge of the table stirring his tea, and his eyes rested on her with amused questioning.

"You take me at face value, don't you—just as you accept your aunt and Marthe and even the egregious M. Bergerac?"

"I've never known any other way," she said simply and his mouth softened.

"No, I suppose you haven't. Shall we try to teach you a few values, Bunny and I?" She looked surprised and a little puzzled and he added inconsequently: "You look like a little girl sitting there in your long blue dressing-gown, a little girl meant for simple, homely pleasures—farm-house teas, birthday cakes with candles, and a bosom to cry on when you're tired."

His words had an unexpected nostalgic beauty for Sabina and her eyes grew bright.

"How strange for you to talk like that," she said and his eyebrows lifted.

"Why? Do you suppose I've never wanted such things myself?"

"Have you never had them?"

"I suppose in some measure—when I was small."

"And a bosom to weep on, too?"

"No, perhaps not—and that's the most important, isn't it?"

It was a strange conversation and somehow out of character with what she knew of him.

"You had Bunny," she said, remembering that his parents had been separated, but he replied with a touch of dryness:

"Bunny was the governess. She had very proper ideas of what was her place. We came to know each other at a much later date."

She was silent, recognising with surprise a childhood much akin to her own. Did a ghost of the lonely little boy still hide behind that indifferent façade, she wondered? Could he be reached by tenderness or had he dwelt so long with his cold loves, the mountains, that he no more desired a bosom to weep upon when he was tired?

"What were you thinking?" he asked, watching the betrayal of her thoughts in the face she had turned to the strengthening morning light, but she could not say these things to him yet. Their acquaintance was still no more than that, and he too arrogant to permit trespass.

"I was thinking—" she began, searching for words, "I —I was remembering that I had meant to take some tea to Bunny as a surprise."

His smile was a little sceptical, but he only fetched another cup and saucer and poured out some fresh tea.

"Here you are," he said. "Then you'd better go and get dressed, and I'll do likewise. Mrs. Cheadle will be here soon to do the fires, unless they're snowed up in the village."

"Do you think they might be?" Sabina asked, standing there in her long blue robe, Bunny's cup in her hands.

"No, of course not," he replied, exasperated by such a literal question, then he smiled.

"Were you thinking we wouldn't get to Penruthan?" he said as if he were rallying a child. "It takes more snow than this to make the roads impassable, my dear."

She remembered that he had promised to take her to see Penruthan today, but she no longer wanted to be reminded of the house which bound her to an unknown man.

"It doesn't matter," she said. "About going to Penruthan, I mean. I can see it another time."

His eyebrows rose, but he made no comment, and she went out of the kitchen, holding the cup of tea carefully in one hand while she hitched up her trailing robe in the other.

Bunny was sympathetic about the death of the robin, but like Brock, she did not encourage sentiment.

"It would have died anyhow, I fear. This weather takes toll of many birds," she said.

"That's what Brock said, but he fed it through the night and kept it warm even though he knew it would die. Don't you think that's strange?"

"I've no doubt it was for your sake."

"Mine?"

"He thought you would grieve. He told me last night that it would be kinder to put the little thing out of its misery."

"Oh!" said Sabina and reflected on what a contradictory person he was, doing his best to keep the bird alive until morning to save her disappointment, but insisting, later on, upon driving her to Penruthan although he knew she was reluctant to go. But when breakfast was finished and he suggested that she got dressed for the drive, she had no ready excuse, since only yesterday she had been so eager, and indeed her blood clamoured to be out in the snow and the sunshine.

"Couldn't we go for a walk, instead?" she asked lamely when he had brought the car round to the door, but his grin was unsympathetic.

"I'm not much of a walker these days with this stiff leg of mine," he said. "Don't you want to see your inheritance by daylight? It's worth a visit, I assure you."

"Yes, of course," she agreed hurriedly, aware that his insistence was not entirely on her account. But when the steep moorland road had taken them over the crest of the moor and Brock turned the car between a pair of massive broken gates, she forgot her strange reluctance and caught her breath sharply.

"I told you it was worth a visit," said Brock.

CHAPTER SIX

PENRUTHAN rose majestic and beautiful from its snowy terraces. Even to Sabina's untrained eye, the house had gracious proportions, and the icicles which hung sparkling from cornice and window gave it the look of a fairy-tale palace. The grounds had fallen into decay, she supposed, remembering the broken steps and balustrade of the other night, but all neglect was hidden and the worn grace of plinth and pillar borrowed fresh beauty from the snow.

"It's lovely," Sabina sighed, feasting her eyes, "and somehow not quite real."

"Snow lends most things a magic touch," Brock replied, watching her eyes grow bright with wonder. "Penruthan, stripped of its disguise, is in a bad state of repair. Here's the key. Take a look round inside but have a care for crumbling floorboards."

He handed her a great iron key with elaborate scrolling, and she hesitated.

"I don't feel I should. It seems like trespassing," she said.

"On your own property? Don't be so foolish."

"Aren't you coming, too?"

"No. Isn't that what you wanted—to see Penruthan for the first time alone?"

She thought she detected a faint taunt in his words and she walked to the massive door between the two tall pillars which formed a porch, and scooped the frozen snow from the keyhole. But she could not turn the key and had to call to Brock.

The door swung inwards slowly under his hands and she saw a great hall soaring to the roof, its dimness cut by a ray of sunlight slanting from a window out of her vision. Motes danced like a cloud of midges in the light and the smell of ancient things filled the emptiness.

"Come with me," she said.

"Afraid of ghosts?" he mocked, but he followed her into the house and left the door open behind them.

Sabina stood in the centre of the hall, feeling small and insignificant, not knowing where to begin. Open doors gave vistas of high, dim rooms, and a wide staircase of stone with heavily carved balustrades led to a gallery and the rooms beyond.

"It's so *big*," Sabina kept repeating. "Who could ever live here in these days?"

"No one probably, unless they were prepared to turn the place into a school or—a hotel."

"Yes, I can see Tante's point. But even if it hadn't been entailed, one would have had a job to sell it, I should think."

"But the Bergeracs would still have been your best market, I presume."

She glanced up at his dark face and felt a passing pity for Tante, cheated from the start in offering her niece a home; poor Tante with her gaiety and her love of good things, forever tormented by a source of revenue which could not be realised.

"Well, aren't you going to make a start on your tour of inspection?" Brock's voice was impatient and she went into the first room she came to.

It was, she supposed, a kind of salon, for its proportions seemed vast and the parquet floor was made for dancing. An old grand piano still stood in splendid isolation, its worn, shabby case painted and scrolled in the Empire style.

"The future ballroom of the Bergerac English branch, perhaps?" observed Brock, and she felt he was laughing at her.

They went from room to room, Brock's dragging footsteps loud on the polished floors. He seemed to know his way about the house and surprised her with knowledge about the original uses of many of the rooms.

"Have you been here before?" she asked him, and he replied carelessly:

"Oh, yes. Most people in these parts have wandered round the place since it's been empty. Penruthan used to be one of the show houses of the Duchy, you know."

"I suppose it was. I'd no idea it was so grand. Madame Bergerac's own family must have been rich too."

"On the contrary, they were rather poor, and only lived in one wing," he said. "I believe the house has always been a bit of a white elephant. It would have saved a lot of trouble if old René Bergerac had been allowed to do what he wanted."

The rooms led one from another in gracious sequence. Some were shuttered, and Brock would undo the bolts to let in the daylight, dislodging dust and cobwebs as he did so. The rooms were empty for the most part, with a stale, piercing cold and the indescribable flavour of gentle decay, but in others there was still furniture, chairs of faded damask, and old presses, pocked with worm.

"I never knew there was furniture," Sabina said, opening an empty cabinet to inspect a dead spider inside. "I wonder why these things were left here."

"Not worth a dealer's trouble, perhaps," Brock answered carelessly. "This room is rather charming, Sabina, and it has a secret cupboard which should appeal."

He showed her how the spring operated in the worm-eaten panelling, but her interest was no more than polite. She had seen an *armoire* which seemed to be a replica of the one which Bunny had in her living-room.

"Look, Brock," she said; "it's the same, surely?"

"The same as what?" he asked, but his voice was absent.

"The *armoire* Bunny has. You told me it was made by someone famous. There can't be many like it, can there?"

"It was one of a pair," he said and she looked at him inquiringly.

"You mean Bunny's *armoire* came from Penruthan?"

He looked annoyed, as if he had not meant her to know.

"It was bought for her by a friend when the stuff was sold," he said shortly. "The other one must have got missed, or else your aunt didn't know the value of a Boulle."

"Tante? You mean *Tante* was selling things from Penruthan?"

"Well, she couldn't sell the house, could she? Not very much was left here, but there was some valuable stuff. Have you no banking account, Sabina, where such proceeds would be lodged?"

Her clear eyes widened with a look of strain.

"No," she replied, "I thought Penruthan was just an empty house. Tante never discussed these things."

"But the contents, as well as the house, were yours," he said gently. "There should be a nice little cache stowed away for you somewhere."

"If Tante sold things without telling me, then it was only to help with the expense I must have been to her," she said coldly.

Her coat had a little collar of cheap fur which Marthe herself would have scorned, but it framed her face with delicate softness in the dim light, and her cheekbones, stained with sudden colour, stood out sharply against the pale confusion of her hair. Brock made a move towards her, but at the altered expression in his face she turned suddenly to run and put a foot straight through the rotten boards he had warned her of.

She cried out with the sudden pain and his arms were round her at once, dragging her back from the treacherous woodwork.

"I never knew anyone with such an instinct for running away," he said, holding her closely. "Did you think I was going to assault you—or something equally silly?"

"I—I don't know," she whispered, ashamed and conscious of her quickening blood at the same time.

But his face altered again as he looked down at her, and he put a hand behind her head, forcing it back, and very deliberately kissed her.

"It seems you were right," he said softly." Now what have you to say?"

She had not struggled; she did not struggle now but stood staring up at him, her lips a little parted and the colour flooding her face. She had nothing to say at all.

The silence of the house settled about them and the faint, protesting creaks of the rotting floor-boards were clearly audible.

"Is that the first time you've been kissed?" he asked, and when she did not reply, let her go abruptly and turned away.

"Well," he said with a return to his old manner, "you can chalk it up as a preparation for M. Bergerac. Have

98

you had enough of this mausoleum or do you want to see upstairs?"

"No," she said suddenly hating Penruthan and all it stood for, "I'd like to go."

It was a relief, she felt, to get out into the sunlight and see the shadows on the snow and the clear sky overhead. Penruthan should go back to the Bergeracs, but she herself would never live here to be reminded of the happenings of today.

She was very silent as they drove home and Brock apparently had no inclination to put her at her ease. For him, of course, such incidents were a commonplace. Had Bunny not warned her that he had an eye for an elegant woman? But no one, thought Sabina ruefully, could describe her as that, and she remembered more sombrely Marthe's prediction that when a man is bored he will amuse himself with anyone that offers . . .

On the high ground it was beginning to thaw where the sun lay hottest, and the icy road seemed more slippery, or else Brock was driving with less regard for caution. Several times Sabina felt the car skid and as they rounded a bend on the hill which led down to Truan, a flock of sheep crossed the road, looking dirty and draggled against the snow.

"Look out!" Sabina cried and instinctively pulled at his arm. He braked too suddenly at the same moment and the car turned in a sharp skid, circled twice and finished up with two wheels in the snow-filled ditch beyond the edge of the moor.

"Get out!" snapped Brock, leaning across her to tug at the door. For a moment the car rocked as if it would turn over completely, then the wheels stuck and Sabina slid out at an angle into a drift of snow.

Brock beside her pulled her out with no gentle grip.

"Haven't you been taught never to interfere with the driver?" he demanded furiously. "You might have landed up in a worse mess, or at best killed a few of those damned sheep."

"I'm sorry," she said, brushing the snow from her hair with nervous fingers. "I didn't even know I had touched you. Was it really my fault?"

"I probably braked too violently as well, but never in any circumstances do such a thing again," he said; then noticed the whiteness of her face.

"You're all right, aren't you?" he asked sharply.

"Yes, I'm all right," she said. "You frightened me more than the accident did."

"Serve you right," he retorted unfeelingly. "You've caused a lot of trouble in your own quiet way, haven't you, young woman? Picking up strangers in pubs, losing yourself on the moor, inviting overtures in an empty house, and now this."

"Since you've brought it up, it wasn't I who invited overtures," she said indignantly, and he grinned.

"Wasn't it? If you hadn't turned to run and fallen through the floor we might still be inspecting the upper rooms of your property—or do you feel that might have led to greater indiscretion?"

"I think you're hateful!" she replied, the colour back in her face. "I think a man who—who kisses a girl and then taunts her with it is—is unspeakable."

"Quite right, he is," he said. "But I wasn't really taunting you, Sabina—didn't you like being kissed? All right, all right—I'm not going to do it again on the public highway."

She had backed away from him hastily, and as he finished speaking she lost her footing and fell into the ditch again.

*   *   *

He stood looking down at her without immediately offering to help her up. His annoyance seemed to have gone.

"You see? Pride goes before a fall," he said. "That should teach you not to anticipate gestures of affection before they happen to you."

"Was it a—a gesture of affection?" she asked.

"What else?"

"I thought perhaps it was just—amusement."

"Oh, I see. Has my good preceptress been dropping timely hints?"

"Not in that way, but Marthe—"

"Oh, that coarse old trollop!"

She sat in the snow, blinking up at him shyly. With her long legs and smooth, rounded forehead she looked like a child who has taken an unexpected tumble, and he reached down to pull her up, this time with gentleness.

"You're very sweet, Sabina Lamb," he said. "A lamb too young for the market, I think."

"I'm only inexperienced," she said with grave sedateness. "One grows up quickly with a little help, I think— even for the market."

His eyes narrowed, and she was struck again by their strange icy blue; the eyes of a mountaineer.

"And I wonder what you mean by that," he said softly. "M. Bergerac may have quite a surprise in store for him, after all."

She turned away. Was he always deliberate in bringing things back to René Bergerac, she wondered? Was he warning her or mocking at the path Tante had chosen for her?

"What do we do about the car?" she asked to change the subject, and he laughed.

"What do you imagine we do, my innocent? We walk. The thing will need a breakdown gang to heave it out of the ditch."

Walk! It was a long way back to the rectory, and Brock with his stiff leg found walking difficult.

"Does that disconcert you?" he asked, seeing the dismay in her face.

"No, but you—won't you stay with the car and let me go to the village for help?" she said, and saw his expression freeze at once into one of arrogant distaste.

"Certainly not," he said brusquely. "I may be a cripple in your eyes, my child, but I can still get around. You will have to suit your pace to mine, that's all."

She flushed scarlet, remembering that Bunny had told her he was afraid of pity. She said no more but started to walk beside him down the hill, aware of his cold withdrawal.

It was an unhappy finish to a confusing morning, she thought, walking the slow miles home. It was a lonely road, and in this weather nothing passed them. She tried to avert her eyes from Brock's halting gait, but it worried

101

her to glimpse the twinge of pain in his face when he slipped and know that this heavy going through the snow was wearing him down. She could have helped, she knew, by lending her shoulder as support, but she did not dare touch him or even suggest a periodical rest. At last he called a halt himself, and when with relief she watched him prop himself against a wall, she saw his eyes upon her.

"Don't look so worried," he said quite pleasantly. "Such occasions are tedious, but I make out in the end."

"I feel I'm to blame," she said because she did not like to ask him if he was in pain.

"Forget it. My careless braking was really the trouble. I suppose I was human enough to demand a scapegoat," he replied. "I'm sorry if I scared you."

Her mouth curved into the tender crescent that Bunny found so endearing and the uncertainty left her face.

"I didn't mind," she said. "It always helps to blast someone, doesn't it?"

He smiled.

"I suppose it does. And do you ever blast anyone, Sabina?"

"Oh, yes, sometimes. Marthe when she makes me feel a fool and people in buses who tread on your toes."

"Tell me about your childhood after your aunt adopted you," he said, and turned to walk on.

Because she thought it would help to distract his attention from his infirmity, she gave him a meticulous account of the life she had led, but she did not feel it could make very interesting hearing to a man of Brock's experience. The cheap schools had been dull, even to her, and the hotels were all the same; only Tante gave colour to those years, with her wit and gaiety, the elegance of her clothes, the bright quirks of her restless mind.

"My father probably wouldn't have approved of Tante making herself responsible for me," Sabina said, laughing. "We were all very English, you see, and Tante had a slight flavour of wickedness because she was French."

"Then why didn't your father make proper arrangements in his lifetime?"

"I don't know. He was a very absent-minded man; and besides, I don't really think there would have been anyone else. Marthe used to say Tante saved me from an institution, but I don't suppose that was true."

"H'm . . . And when was the rich M. Bergerac thought of as a solution to everyone's problems?"

"When I was sixteen or seventeen, I suppose, though I don't think Tante started negotiations then."

"You're sure the negotiations, as you call them, aren't principally in your aunt's mind?"

"Well, not now, you forget she's staying at the Château Berger."

"So she is. And M. Bergerac is being gently persuaded, according to plan."

She glanced at him quickly.

"That doesn't sound very flattering. I understood he is in need of a wife as well as the house and is quite agreeable to discuss the arrangement."

"Led up the garden by a photograph of spurious glamour?"

Sabina flushed at his tone and wondered if Brock and René had ever met and discussed the project.

"Yes, the photograph was a mistake," she agreed. "But Tante says it will not matter that I am rather plain, for M. Bergerac would not care for a wife who might turn the heads of his clients."

"I see. And do you consider yourself plain?"

She sighed, then answered prosaically:

"Well, I am rather. My eyes are too big for my face, my forehead too bulgy and my hair never made up its mind whether to be blonde or just near-mouse."

He slipped a hand through her arm, whether from a gesture of friendliness or for the support for which he would not ask, she did not know, but it made her happy.

"The French would describe it as *cendré*— far more subtle than plain blonde," he told her. "You haven't been allowed much conceit of yourself, have you, Sabina? Well, a man can doubtless teach you that more successfully than a smart French aunt."

"Oh!" She did not know what to reply to this and he had made her suddenly shy. He had taught her already, she thought wryly, to be conscious of an inadequate wardrobe and a lack of feminine tricks which she had never before been called upon to use.

"You know," he said with a touch of his old mockery, "it's very odd that you should always allude to your future husband so formally."

"Well, I've never met him; besides—he's never seemed quite real, to tell you the truth. When I think of M. Bergerac, I see someone in tails and a white waistcoat, very polite with shiny hair—like the head waiters in our hotels."

"Good God!" he exclaimed.

"Isn't he like that? You say you've met him."

"Not very, I hope."

"Oh! He's attractive, then?"

"Not at all," said Brock crisply, "but since he's his father's son and the name of Bergerac still means something in France, there are plenty who like to boast of his acquaintance."

"Oh!" she said again. "It doesn't sound as if he's going to find me very satisfactory."

"On the contrary, he will probably find you a relief after the sycophantic women he has to deal with," he said, then added slyly, "Besides, a biddable, wisely brought up young wife will be a protection. Hasn't your aunt told you that?"

"Ye-s, but—"

"But what?"

"Well, nothing really. I'm getting muddled."

He made no reply and seemed to lose interest in the subject. She had been talking too much and too inconsequently, she thought, seeing the weariness in his face. He leant on her now without apology and she found it difficult to match her steps to his in the shifting snow. He knew of a short cut which would take them across one of the moorland tracks to the churchyard, thus saving a mile, but it must have been a gruelling couple of hours for him.

"You should have waited with the car," she said as the litle graveyard was at last in sight and she saw the effort it was now costing him to keep going.

"Perhaps I should," he agreed with surprising meekness. "I shall be infernally crippled tomorrow."

"Like Mrs. Cheadle's bad legs," giggled Sabina, able

104

for the first time to make a small jest about his infirmity and see him grin.

"Yes, it must be. Mrs. Cheadle and I will have to get together and discuss our ailments."

"You," said Sabina, feeling emboldened by his response, "will rest by the fire and take orders, and not make people feel that they are trespassing when they only want to help."

He paused in sight of the house to look down at her.

"Do I do that?" he asked with surprise.

"Yes, you do. Look how you bit off my head when I suggested earlier on that you should stay behind. Bunny says—"

"What does Bunny say?"

"Nothing that I should repeat."

"I'm sorry if I bit off your head," he said mildly. "You should have bitten back."

"Yes," she said, considering the matter seriously, "but Tante and Marthe have never encouraged pert answers and I haven't much practice."

He walked on again but made an effort to lean upon her arm less heavily.

"It would appear that I've been taking an unfair advantage," he said. "All right, Sabina, for the next few days I'll take the place of the robin for you. I shall probably be glad of solicitude."

"The robin?" she inquired, not following his allusion.

"Something to be responsible for, something that needs you—don't you remember?"

"Yes," she said, knowing suddenly that she desired this of him with aching intensity. "But you would never need me, Brock. You don't need anyone—only the mountains."

"And second best isn't good enough?"

They were walking between the graves now, and she brushed the snow tenderly from one of the headstones.

"Oh, no," she replied, "second best isn't as chilly as it sounds and I haven't been brought up to expect the best."

"Sometimes you make me want to shake you," he said impatiently, but he did not alarm her any more.

"Well, you did when you found me that night at Penruthan," she said demurely. "If it makes you feel better you can do it again."

"You're learning fast, aren't you?" he said, and observed the tiredness in her small face. "I'm sorry, my dear; I'm afraid I've been inconsiderate for the last mile or so. You're scarcely used to country endurances or the weight of a six-foot man. Are you hungry? I'm afraid we've missed our lunch, but no doubt Bunny can find us something."

But Bunny, Sabina felt, was disapproving. She listened to the tale of their misfortune with pursed lips and gave Sabina a look which said plainly that she knew who was to blame for the whole affair.

"Any undue strain on that leg sets up a peck of trouble," she said, snatching plates out of the oven where she had been keeping something hot against their return. "Brock can suffer a lot of pain from that injury."

Sabina felt reproved and guilty of a lack of adult firmness.

"I should have insisted he stayed with the car, I suppose," she said, "but it's difficult to know with Brock."

"Well, it can't be helped," Bunny replied, not responding to a plea which she would normally have understood. "You will be able to see for yourself the folly of pretending a disability doesn't exist. You'd better keep out of his way for the next few days, Sabina. Brock can be difficult when his leg troubles him excessively."

*   *   *

But Brock was not difficult. In the days that followed, although he was clearly suffering a fair amount of pain, he seemed content to sit by the fire, his leg propped on a stool, while Sabina sewed and Bunny made periodical appearances from the kitchen or other parts of the house where she was occupied.

"Tell me some of your funny rhymes," he would say, and she would search her memory for the jingles which had comforted her in childhood because when there was no one to talk to reciting aloud to an imaginary audience provided company.

She would say for him *The King of China's Daughter*, and Ben Jonson's Battle-Hymn for James the First, and

Pigsnye and a whole bunch of singing rhymes and old street cries. He liked particularly:

> *Young lambs to sell, white lambs to sell;*
> *If I'd as much money as I could tell*
> *I wouldn't be crying, Young lambs to sell!*

"That should have been written for you," he commented lazily, and she blushed and would not repeat the catch next time he asked for it.

"Where did you learn all these things?" he inquired curiously.

"I had an old book full of queer odds and ends that the other children didn't seem to know," she said. "Willie knows rhymes, too. He's only just started saying them for me."

"Poor Willie! The most popular rhyme in these parts used to be the one the children made up about him," said Brock idly, and Sabina's eyes darkened.

She remembered walking to the village one morning and meeting Willie followed by a handful of small children who suddenly burst into a jeering ditty sung to the tune of Bobby Shafto . . .

> *Willie Washer's proper mazed,*
> *Doesn't know where he was raised.*
> *Silly Willie, proper dazed,*
> *Silly Willie Wash-er!*

At the last line the boy had turned to give chase, his arms waving wildly and his gentle face distorted with rage. Willie was turned sixteen now, but the old taunt could still make him lose all control of himself.

"Children are very cruel," Sabina said, and Brock raised an eyebrow.

"Oh, I don't know. Most of them are just unthinking little animals," he said. "The race goes to the strong, you know. Willie and other maimed creatures are natural butts."

There was a trace of bitterness in his voice, and Sabina said gently and a little shyly:

"The maimed might be special, I think. If you have something—physical to put up with, it could make you—well, more tolerant of others."

"Do you think so? Well, if you're speaking personally,

107

Sabina, you should know by now that I'm not the most tolerant of people."

"No, but—"

"But what?"

"In your mind I think you are."

"What's the difference? You really are very young and very white, aren't you, Miss Lamb? Much too young to be for sale," he said, but she did not mind his derision, for she did not think he meant it.

It was a strange few days Sabina reflected, now so far in thought from Tante and Marthe and the cheap hotels that she could regard the rectory as home. It froze hard at nights and the snow was slow to go although no more fell. After that first sunny day, the wind blew bitterly and the three of them seemed marooned in an intimate fastness while ice blurred the windows and the milk each day was frozen in the pans before Bunny set them for scalding.

There was plenty to keep Sabina busy in the mornings, for Mrs. Cheadle would not risk her ulcers this weather to walk up from the village, but in the quiet afternoons when she sat by the fire, sewing or mending for Bunny, she would love to idle over her work while she watched the flames leap up the cavernous chimney, and listened to the high wind sweeping round the house. Of Tante at the Château Berger she had heard nothing. Even she, like M. Bergerac, had become a little unreal, and Marthe, with her friends in London, although she had sent Sabina clothes, had not written.

Brock would lie back in his chair and watch Sabina through half-closed eyes. Often she would think he was asleep, but sometimes, when she let her own gaze dwell on his dark, saturnine face, he would open his eyes and disconcert her with a pertinent remark. She wondered about the accident which had deprived him of his old life, and once she asked him shyly how it had happened.

"On a climb," he told her briefly." I fell and got a compound fracture of the knee. Exposure didn't help it to mend. Silly, wasn't it?"

But he seemed less inclined to talk about the mountains than before, and would turn the conversation into more personal channels, commenting idly on what she wore and grinning when he made her blush.

He did not care for Tante's outworn dresses, which had been her portion since she was adult enough to wear them.

"Too old for you," he would say, frowning. "And too sophisticated. You aren't the type for slinky lines and daring *décolletage*."

"It was very expensive," she protested on that occasion, and dragged the slipping neckline higher on her throat. "The trouble is I haven't the figure for well-cut clothes—Tante has often said so."

"Tante would," he remarked dryly. "Does she never buy you clothes of your own?"

"Well, of ocurse, only it seems silly to spend money when her own things are still quite good."

"And is the dyspeptic M. Bergerac to be introduced to his future bride wearing a cast-off wardrobe?"

"He's not dyspeptic," she retorted, goaded as usual by his disrespectful reference to René Bergerac,"—at least, I don't think so. When M. Bergerac comes back with Tante I'm to have a little trousesau."

"Will you start collecting it in Cornwall?" he asked politely and she laughed.

"Of course not. When the time comes, Tante will write to Marthe, I suppose, and I will have to go back."

But he did not always tease her. If he was not prepared to discuss her proposed marriage with any seriousness, he encouraged chatter about herself. She thought he must have learnt a great deal about her in their short acquaintance, and did not find it strange that she knew so little of him. She did not know his business, or, indeed, if he had one, and it did not occur to her to ask. Men, Tante had always said, told one what was necessary; it was both impertinent and unwise to inquire into masculine affairs. Bunny would answer questions about Brock's boyhood, of which she liked to talk, but she was evasive if more recent times were touched on and Sabina came to the conclusion that Marthe had probably been right; Brock had little money, possibly an ill-paid job, and stayed with his old governess because he had nowhere else to go.

By the end of the week the snow had nearly gone. The skies were grey and an icy wind still rattled the doors and windows of the rectory, but Brock seemed better. His face had ceased contracting with a sudden twinge of pain when he moved and he began to talk vaguely of leaving Truan.

"You are going?" exclaimed Sabina with such dismay that he smiled.

"Well, not just yet; but I'm only here on a visit, like you," he said.

It was a sharp reminder of the impermanence of her holiday, and she realised then how much these past few days had done to make her forget her obligations. Brock had been gentle and Bunny had treated her as if she really belonged, but it was an interlude in her life just as it was in theirs, though for her so much more important.

"Come here," said Brock suddenly from his chair by the fire and held out a hand.

He and Sabina had been left together for tea, for it was Bunny's afternoon again for the Women's Institute. Tea was finished, but neither of them had troubled to light the lamp.

Sabina crossed the room slowly and sat on the floor in the firelight, and Brock touched her cheek.

"You like it here, don't you?" he said. "Bunny will keep you for as long as you like, you know."

But that, she thought, would not be quite the same. She was fond of Bunny, but it was Brock who, for all his uncomfortable ways, had given her this sense of sanctuary.

"Bunny has been most kind," she answered politely, "but Tante must return soon. It's nearly a month since she's been gone."

"Your aunt wouldn't be averse to another month in the luxury of the Château Berger, I imagine."

"No, but you forget—"

"I do *not* forget the egregious M. Bergerac," he said irritably, "but it would seem that he has been only too happy to allow Madame board and lodging for so long as she pleases. The negotiations are doubtless progressing with leisure and much finesse on both sides."

She glanced at him warily, suspecting, for not the first time, that he knew more of Tante's affairs than he would admit.

"There is the question of money," Sabina said, remembering the matter much too late. "It's odd that Tante has sent me none. Bunny isn't well off. I—I can't live here on her charity."

"There's no need to worry. Bunny and your aunt are in communication."

"Oh, I see." Sabina felt relieved. It would have been typical of Tante to forget inconvenient obligations should her own resources run low.

"You worry about a lot of things that shouldn't concern you, don't you?" he said. "I think you must be very conscientious."

He was idly twisting a strand of her hair round his finger and she leant against his chair, conscious of a new intimacy.

"Brock," she said, "is it wrong to marry a man you don't love?"

A fortnight ago she could never have brought herself to ask him such a question, but she did not fear his mockery now.

"It depends what you want out of life," he answered lazily. "Riches and ease with fat M. Bergerac, or love in a cottage, which can be very uncomfortable."

"Fat?"

"Well, he could be fat. Good living makes you flabby."

"Oh!"

"But you've never had very romantic ideas about our mutual friend, have you? Very polite with shiny hair, looking like a head waiter, I think you said."

He was teasing her, of course, but it was strange he could never describe satisfactorily a man he had met.

"Well, you told me he wasn't at all like that," she said.

"And I also told you he wasn't in the least attractive," he retorted bluntly. "You hadn't got these doubts when you first came here."

"I hadn't met any other men then," she said and immediately blushed at what her words must imply.

"You know," he said slowly, "that remark could be taken as a direct invitation. I think Bunny's very trusting to leave us alone together in the circumstances."

"But she knows—she knows—" she stammered helplessly, and he grinned.

"That I wouldn't make love to you, were you going to

111

say? She knows nothing of the sort—in fact she might nearly approve in her prim spinsterish fashion."

"What nonsense!"

"Nothing of the kind. Experience is good for everyone, as she would be the first to tell you."

"Experience for your amusement wouldn't help me at all," she said and tried to move away from him, but he had her suddenly by the shoulders, lifting her up on her knees so that her face was level with his.

"I amuse myself with adult women, not with children," he said grimly. "Which category do you prefer to be in?"

"I'm not a child," Sabina said, the colour staining her cheekbones.

"No, you're not," he replied softly and kissed her deliberately for the second time.

She slid back on to her heels and rested her head against his knee wanting to weep. It was not fair of Tante to explain so little, she thought . . . it was not right of Marthe to dismiss so much . . . She felt Brock's hand on her head and gently he slipped it down under her chin to raise her face.

"You'll find out for yourself it's wrong to marry a man you don't love," he said strangely. "You have very few defences, my little lamb, should they be put to the test."

She stared at him mutely. She had not even known until now that defences were necessary.

He saw the brightness of tears on her lashes and brushed them away.

"Would you go through with this marriage if you found yourself in love with another man?" he asked.

She wondered if he meant to be cruel and answered steadily:

"I have no choice until I'm twenty-one."

"And then?"

"I don't know. I—I'm so far committed."

His eyebrows met on a quick frown.

"Only by your aunt. You are as free as any other girl if you have the courage."

His hand was warm on her slender throat and she lowered her lashes.

112

"I don't think I would need courage if I was sure," she said.

"Of yourself?"

"No—of him."

He released her as they heard Bunny's key in the front door, and Sabina moved away, conscious of her hot cheeks and wet lashes.

Bunny stood in the doorway and surveyed them, her quick eyes resting longest on Sabina's face in the firelight. In her old-fashioned coat and little pork-pie hat she looked prim and slightly severe.

"Do you not want a light?" she asked, and made the question sound like a rebuke.

Sabina jumped up to find the matches but Bunny forestalled her and lighted the lamp, turning up the wick with precision.

"And how was the Institute?" Brock asked lazily.

"There were very few there," Bunny replied, automatically straightening ornaments on the mantelshelf. "Too cold, I expect, and the roads are still bad. Have you finished with the tea-things?"

"I'll wash them up," said Sabina quickly, glad to get out of the room, and she lifted the tray and took it out to the kitchen.

"It's not fair, Brock," Bunny said as the door closed.

He raised his eyebrows but did not reply, and she stood there, her slightly protuberant teeth pressing into her underlip.

"I heard from Mrs. Lamb this morning" she said. "She seems well satisfied with the progress of her arrangements. Are you going to allow this farce to continue?"

"Perhaps it is ceasing to be a farce," he said gently. "You never did care for intrigue, did you, Bunny?"

"I've most likely seen too much of it," she replied shortly. "I've grown fond of that child, Brock. I wouldn't like to see her get hurt."

"And what about me? I always thought I was your favourite pupil."

"Oh, you!" she exclaimed, sounding unusually exasperated. "You can look after yourself—you're a grown man."

"True," he admitted. "But what about those little lectures you are fond of reading me?"

"I've told you before," she said, "that there are other ways of fulfilment than casual affairs, and Sabina is not like the others."

"No, she isn't, but that should please, rather than alarm you."

She undid her coat with fingers which suddenly shook a little.

"If I thought for a moment you had more serious intentions—" she began and he grinned at her.

"What would you do? Acquaint Madame that her scheme was in danger? Advise her to bring M. Bergerac speedily to the point?"

"Oh, you're impossible!" she exclaimed, sounding really cross. "If I'd known—if I'd thought—"

"But you did think, my dissembling Bunny," he retorted gently. "You had one or two schemes of your own, I think, when you agreed to take in our little waif and stray. Now you are involved in intrigue whether you like it or not."

She stood there for another moment, indecisive and thoroughly upset, then she quickly left the room to remove her outdoor clothes.

CHAPTER SEVEN

SLEET fell in the night, but by morning it had turned to rain, and Sabina wakened to see the graves in the little churchyard once more uncovered and desolate in the steady downpour. It was not a cheerful sight, she thought, and shivered.

She had not slept well. She had lain for a long time, looking at Brock's mountains in the lamplight, and remembering that Bunny had told her they were his only love. Had he known when he kissed her that then she would grow up; that never again could she laugh at the rich M. Bergerac and accept his being with such childlike unconcern? Was she, away from Tante's and Marthe's stern seclusion, in danger of falling in love with the first experienced stranger who had shown her a little attention, or was she simply like the young chambermaids in the hotel who lost their heads to anyone because, after all, it was necessary to be loved and needed?

She dropped to sleep at last with her lamp still burning, and by morning the oil had run out.

"I'm sorry," she told Bunny nervously, for going to sleep with one's light on had been a crime in Marthe's thrifty eye. "I wasn't reading, I—I just went to sleep before I expected to."

Bunny observed the shadows under her eyes but made no comment. She herself was quiet and uncommunicative all that day, and by evening it became evident that she was in for a cold.

"Oh, dear!" she said with exasperation; "and I get such bad ones. I'm afraid—I'm very much afraid it may mean taking to my bed."

But she fought hard to remain up and about, as if, thought Sabina guiltily, she was loth to leave her two guests unchaperoned by day. The house reeked of eucalyptus, and Bunny's nose got pinker and her speech thicker and the next day she was obliged to give in.

"It's inconsiderate to spread your germs about," Brock told her unfeelingly. "You'll only pass them on to Sabina and me."

"But there's the cooking," she protested feebly.

"Can you cook, Sabina?" Brock asked.

"W-ell—" Sabina began doubtfully, but at sight of Bunny's poor mottled face she said quickly: "Of course. We'll manage, Bunny dear, and I shall enjoy bringing up your meals on neat little trays with pretty cloths."

"Well, dear, if you think you *could* manage for a day or two perhaps I would be wise . . . Mrs. Cheadle is coming in the mornings again and—I really do long to get my head down on a pillow . . ."

Sabina took charge at once, delighted that she could be of help. She insisted on lighting a fire in Bunny's room and sent Brock out for coal and wood, despite the governess's protest that this was an extravagance; bottles were filled and hot drinks prepared and by the time Bunny was tucked up in bed she looked quite dazed.

"This is spoiling," she said, watching the fire, which had not been lighted for years, burning brightly in the grate. "I've never had anyone to make a fuss of me before —it's rather nice."

Sabina regarded her with affection. Clad in one of her old-fashioned night-gowns and a spencer, with her greying hair in two wispy plaits on her shoulders, she looked quite different and somehow a little pathetic.

"That's how I felt when you looked after me," the girl replied gently. "We should do a bit of spoiling of each other—we're a solitary pair."

"But not you child," said Bunny seriously. "You have all your life before you and you are young and very charming. And Sabina—"

But Bunny finished ambiguously:

"You'll see that Brock is comfortable? A man does not like too much chatter with his meals or—or too much sitting in the firelight with nothing to do."

Sabina's smile was tender.

"Dear Bunny," she said, "I won't worry him with my— my company more than he wants."

Bunny patted her hand.

"That's a good child . . . though I did not mean . . . I was not implying . . ."

"Don't worry about us," Sabina said. "Brock, as you should know, makes his own rules."

"Yes . . . that is what I'm afraid of . . ." Bunny murmured, but she was too stupefied with her cold to finish, and Sabina left her to sleep.

She went downstairs, unsure herself as to what the hours alone with Brock might hold. Bunny's presence was a check on thoughts and embarrassing silences, and Brock, if he thought at all of that other evening, had neither sought Sabina's company nor introduced dangerous topics of conversation.

But for the moment meals were a far more alarming prospect than possible encounters, for Sabina had never so much as boiled an egg. She and Tante had always lived hotel life and if extra cooking had been needed Marthe had taken charge with scant appreciation for the efforts of others. How and with what was Sabina to cook Brock's supper tonight?

He found her an hour later sitting on the kitchen table surrounded by cookery books. Her small face looked more pointed than ever and her eyes were enormous with anxiety as she feverishly scanned the pages of the book in her hand.

"Well!" he observed, "it looks as if you're planning a Lucullan feast. What's it to be—Boeuf à la Mode or Sole Bonne Femme?"

"I haven't decided yet," she said hurriedly. "What do you particularly like?"

"Well, now, let me see . . .grouse—no, that's out of season . . .I have it! How about Arroz Paella alla Valenciana?"

"What on earth's that?"

"A most delectable dish from Spain with exciting ingredients—chicken, lobsters, pimentos, saffron—and, of course, rice."

"Chicken *and* lobster?" protested Sabina her eyes wide with dismay. "Anyway, we haven't any of those things."

"A pity—still it can wait till another day. Well, let's be more humble. What about risotto? That's a simple peasant dish that can be made with practically anything."

"Risotto . . . risotto . . ." Sabina muttered to herself and referred feverishly to the index at the end of the

117

book, but this failed her, for it was one of Bunny's many austerity cookery books, and she pounced on another.

"It doesn't seem to be here, either," she said and Brock raised his eyebrows.

"But surely you will know without having to look it up," he said with grave surprise. "It's only a question of rice and odds and ends and of course the flavouring."

"I forget things," she said, beginning to look a little flushed. "It's easier if I see it written down."

He took the book out of her hand and stood grinning down at her.

"Be honest," he said. "You can't cook at all, can you?"

She knew now he had been teasing her, but she was not going to admit herself beaten. She could not let him open a tin in the last resort of male incompetence in the kitchen, and in all these dog-eared, well-worn books there must be something that could be cooked by just following the instructions. Her mind already reeled with impossible directions . . . *make a roux . . . blanch the kidneys . . . fold in the whites . . .* and clear but alarming, *take twelve eggs . . .*

"Of course I can," she said bravely, meeting his amused eyes with determination, "but I'm rusty. If you leave me alone I'll find something."

"I beg your pardon," he replied. "Well, I'll come and watch you when you begin. I like to see a charming girl busy over the stove."

He went away then and Sabina, hoping that his threat was merely idle, went out to the larder to inspect Bunny's reserves. There were chops and liver and plenty of bacon, and after another consultation with the cookery book she decided on a mixed grill. It was a masculine, English dish, she thought, and it would be easier and just as good fried with plenty of onions and tomatoes.

It took her a long time to prepare and by the time she was ready to cook the sink was piled with dirty plates and sauce-pans. She did not understand the regulating of the stove and got everything too hot, and there did not seem to be enough frying-pans to go round. When Brock, true to his word, sat himself down in a wicker chair to watch, smoke from the hot fat was already filling the kitchen and Sabina had burnt the chops.

"Dear me!" he said, "what are we eating?"

"A mixed grill," she said, "only there aren't enough frying-pans."

"Then why don't you use the grill?"

While she was thinking of a sensible reply to that the liver caught and she turned it over to find it black and hard.

"I wish you'd go away," she said, burning herself with flying fat; "you make me nervous."

"The onions are catching," he pointed out with maddening calm and she turned too sharply to rescue them, upsetting one of the pans on the floor. The hot fat spurted over her and she clasped a hand to her breast in agony.

"Let me look," said Brock, on his feet behind her. "No, don't hold it like that; you'll make it worse. Let me see."

She held out the burnt hand, trying at the same time to stop the tears from falling. He examined it carefully, then went out of the room and returned with Bunny's first-aid box.

He dressed the hand with gentleness and skill, and she stood mutely, watching his strong, well-shaped fingers as he worked. On the kitchen stove, the frying-pans gave forth a villainous smell. The meal was ruined.

"The pain will go quite soon," he said when he had finished. "That dressing has very soothing properties. Cry if you want to. Burns can hurt, I know."

"It's not *that*," she said, fighting back the tears. "It's the s-supper. Everything's b-black."

"Why wouldn't you admit you couldn't cook?" he asked curiously.

"Because you were so superior. I thought there must be something I could manage, even though I'd never done it before."

"A mixed grill transferred to the frying-pan wasn't a very wise choice," he said and began deftly removing the pans to the scullery, where she could hear them sizzling as he ran water into them. He opened the windows to let out the smoke, then cleaned up the stove and adjusted dampers with a practised hand.

"What are we going to eat, now?" she asked with despair. "There's no more meat. I—I could boil eggs, I suppose, but it's a frightful admission of failure."

"You'd better leave the matter of food to me," he said, with a smile.

"Can *you* cook?" she asked, and he nodded. "Then you might have told me what I was doing wrong instead of—instead of sitting there gloating!"

"Poor Sabina! I couldn't resist seeing how you would cope unaided. Never mind, I'll make up for it by serving you with a superb omelette."

"An omelette!" she exclaimed, exasperated. "Why didn't I think of that?"

"It's as well you didn't," he commented dryly. "Omelettes are not for the inexperienced. They require skill and a light touch, or what do you get? A pancake like leather with no delicacy, no lightness and sparkle."

She glanced at him curiously. He had spoken with the creative instinct of an artist, and for one wild moment she wondered if this was what he did for a living. Was he a chef in somebody's restaurant, wearing a tall white cap, or was he somebody famous who lectured on the radio.

He gave her a quizzical look as she laughed a little hysterically, and told her to lay the table.

"We might as well eat in here," he said. "An omelette should go straight from the pan to the table. When you've done that, Bunny's will be ready to take up."

She would have liked to watch the mysterious rite of omelette-making, but he allowed no idling in the kitchen, and she had only just put the finishing touches to Bunny's tray when the first omelette was ready, miraculously golden and fluffy with button mushrooms scattered carelessly round. He put a cover quickly over the plate and told Sabina to hurry.

Bunny's praise was hard to bear.

"Why, Sabina, how professional!" she exclaimed, when she beheld the omelette. "I'd no idea you were a chef—but of course, you were brought up in the French tradition, were you not?"

"I didn't cook it—Brock did," said Sabina miserably and described the ignominious fate of the mixed grill.

120

"Oh, dear, what sinful waste!" was Bunny's first rejoinder, then seeing the girl's crestfallen face, she added kindly, "Never mind, dear, it was a good attempt, but I should leave the cooking to Brock in future, if I were you. He's quite an expert."

"How does he know? I mean it's not usual for a man, is it, unless—unless—?"

Bunny gave her a quick look.

"Unless it's part of his trade?" she asked. "Plenty of men are excellent cooks as a hobby, my dear. Why don't you ask Brock if you're curious as to what he does for a living?"

*   *   *

But she did not ask him. Bunny's retort had seemed rather like a rebuke to Sabina, and it was possible that in her old-fashioned way the governess did not approve of the manner in which her favourite pupil made his living. But tonight such matters had no consequence. It was new and curiously intimate to be feeding in the kitchen with the firelight bright on the flags and the china on the old dresser shedding a warmth of colour in the light of the lamp.

Brock had made coffee in a fashion never achieved by Bunny, and they sat at the table with its coarse, checked cloth, in companionable silence.

"You look like Alice in Wonderland with that ribbon round your hair," he said suddenly and she smiled across at him, conscious that his mood had softened. Perhaps it had done him good to witness her discomfiture and serve a meal that was a rebuke in itself.

"Could you teach me, do you think, to cook?" she asked, and his eyebrows shot up.

"Why should it concern you?" he said. "The wife of René Bergerac will have the finest chef in Europe."

There they were back again, she thought, regretting her question at once. It seemed that at no time, now, could she not be overshadowed by the Château Berger.

"I suppose so," she said disconsolately. "It all sounds—rather wasted on me."

"But you enjoy your food—you will adapt yourself

quickly to the comforts and well-being of such a life. There are many who would envy you."

"I would like," she said, stretching her arms to embrace the room, "my own life . . . my own kitchen . . . a home. A hotel isn't a home, is it?"

"The Château Berger is rather different," he said. "You will have your own wing, I don't doubt, and nothing to stop you having your own kitchen, too, once you can cook."

"You're laughing at me," she said. "Don't you understand what I mean?"

"Oh, yes, but have you thought that M. Bergerac may also have ideas?"

"But he only wants a house and a wife who will be a— a sort of figurehead."

"I imagine he expects more than that," Brock observed dryly. "Did you suppose a marriage of convenience ruled out the normal privileges of a union?"

"No," she said, "but it's difficult to imagine the reactions of a man you've never met, and Tante says he has poor health."

"Don't let that deceive you," he retorted unkindly. "A man has to be in very poor health not to expect his rights."

She left the table and began wandering round the kitchen, opening cupboards and shutting them in an aimless fashion and coming to rest finally on a rough milking-stool by the range.

"If you're trying to warn me, Brock, that I will have the normal obligations to fulfil, I've always known it," she said with dignity, and he pushed back his chair impatiently.

"You make a brave showing," he said, "but you speak with the innocent sureness of inexperience."

"Why should you care?" she returned with spirit. "You aren't responsible for the success or failure I may make of my life."

"True, why should I care?" he replied, but added softly, "except, as I told you, you may get hurt, but that's something that must happen to all of us. One can't guard against life."

She wondered for the first time if he had ever been in love; not with the mountains which had been his solace, but with some woman who had failed to measure up to his standards.

"If you don't love, you are less likely to be hurt," she said firmly and he grinned.

"What appalling cynicism in one so young!" he exclaimed. "Don't you intend to try to love poor M. Bergerac, who has poor health, then?"

"Well—" she said doubtfully, imagining René Bergerac, middle-aged and rather fat, with a weak digestion to say the least of it. The fact that he had been a rake in his youth no longer meant very much. A rake should look like Brock, dark and sure and cynical, with a hard charm that could soften to tenderness when he chose . . .

"It's a shame to tease you, " he said. "Let's get cleared up. You can't wash up with that bandaged hand, but you can dry. Come on."

For the rest of the evening he was noncommittal, commenting acidly on the heap of dirty pans she had left in the sink, but rewarding her with a friendly pat when the last clean plates were stacked.

"Tomorrow," he said with some pleasure, "we will go marketing. If I am to be chef for the next day or so we will have none of Bunny's plain rectory fare. I will show you what to expect when you get to France. Now, what do you think you'll fancy? All the out-of-season things— quail, woodcock, partridge?"

"In a pear-tree?" she asked, and at his mild look of surprise an unwonted gaiety took her, and she danced round the kitchen singing:

On the first day of Christmas, my true love sent to me
A partridge in a pear-tree . . .

"How astonishing!" Brock observed, watching her attentively. "What else did your true love send?"

"Oh, lots of things. Lords a-leaping, ladies dancing, pipers piping, drummers drumming."

"A thoughtful selection, to be sure. Nobody need be bored."

"There were lots more, and to finish up with, three French hens, two turtle doves and—oh, yes, I'd forgotten five gold rings."

"Five? Was he providing for the eventuality of four more husbands, then?"

"Now you've spoilt it," she said, and he gave the ribbon she had tied round her head an affectionate tweak.

"Dear Sabina," he teased, "you do rise delightfully."

"Of course," she amended quite seriously, "there *were* twelve lords a-leaping, so I suppose—"

"You suppose nothing of the kind," he retorted. "True loves are the same all the world over, one love, one ring, one happy ending; isn't that the correct formula? Now I think it's time we packed up and went to bed."

It was a pleasurable few days for Sabina, proud that she had the running of the house in her hands. Willie came into the kitchen, which was unusual for him, and sat by the fire, not speaking, when it was too wet to work outside, and Mrs. Cheadle, although her housework suffered, drank endless cups of tea and was cosily garrulous.

"You've got us all tamed, haven't you, Sabina?" Brock mocked gently. "Even poor Willie is, like the robin, content to nest by the fire."

"Perhaps," she said, "But I don't think you're one of the tamed, Brock."

His eyebrows lifted, but he made no reply and she did not feel any longer that she might be impertinent in teasing him.

He was as good as his word as regards cooking. Sabina watched while delectable dishes formed magically under his supervision, and although he might rap her fingers when he caught them running greedily round the edges of saucepans, he seemed pleased by the awe and respect with which she observed his efforts.

"You're an excellent audience," he told her. "If you never lose that gift you'll have men at your feet all your life."

She giggled, picturing herself with an adoring chain of admirers, and he said severely:

"You underrate yourself, Sabina, as I've told you before. You must learn to command homage as the right of your sex."

"Must I?" she asked, with a sigh, and he grinned.

"Well, perhaps not. I like you as you are."

They continued to have their meals in the kitchen and Sabina was happy, indulging in her own private make-believe. She felt a little guilty when she took up Bunny's tray because she was grateful to the cold which kept her upstairs, but Bunny, although she fretted because she was not about in the mornings to help the daily woman, was grateful too for her respite.

"I must have been more tired than I knew," she told Sabina apologetically, "and it's so nice being waited upon."

Sabina regarded her with affection. In her governessing days, she supposed, Bunny had never been waited upon, and as an impoverished vicar's wife she had done the waiting herself.

"When I marry you must come and stay with me," she said impulsively, and flushed at the governess's faint look of surprise. It was, she supposed, a little presumptuous to extend invitations to the home of a man she had not yet met.

The rain had stopped at last, and on the day Bunny was to come downstairs again, Brock beckoned Sabina out of doors.

"You see? Spring has crept up on us unawares," he said, and she looked about her with astonishment.

The morning air was sweet and softer than silk, and even the moor had stirred from its winter sleep and showed tender colour in its bleakness. The first primroses grew among the graves and the neglected garden had put out spear-like shoots of green.

"Oh . . ." said Sabina softly. "It's like a miracle . . ."

"In the Maritimes—round Venice—it will be still more beautiful," Brock said, but she turned away, not wanting to be reminded of the Château Berger. The little time of felicity was over, she thought. Today Bunny was coming down, and tomorrow life would be as it had been, with no more meals in the kitchen, and an intimacy at once broken by the presence of a third person.

They made a fuss of Bunny, and Sabina particularly, because she was conscious of ingratitude, waited on her in a hundred ways, tucking her on the sofa in the living-room, making the *tisanes* which Marthe had taught her, because as she said, convalescence must go on for a while longer. It lasted, in effect, for another day; then Bunny put on her overall and tied her head up in the unbecoming handkerchief and began a furious round of cleaning and polishing.

"It certainly does not do," she said, "to relinquish the reins, as my dear husband always maintained. Look at the dust in these cabinets and the position of the ornaments—everything in the wrong place."

"I did help Mrs. Cheadle," Sabina said, feeling reproved.

"I know, dear, and it was very kind; but you can't be expected to know where things live, as I do," said Bunny, and her eyes fell on the *armoire*. Ah, now someone *has* cared for that. Was it you, Sabina?"

"Yes," Sabina said. "It's so beautiful, and since I saw the other one at Penruthan, I've taken particular care."

"The other one?" said Bunny vaguely.

"Yes. Brock said they were originally a pair and a friend had bought this one for you."

For some reason Bunny looked flustered.

"Oh, yes, I'd forgotten," she said. "Sabina, I hope you don't think—well, I suppose all that furniture really belonged to you."

"I didn't know of its existence," said Sabina gently. "And if I had—well, I would have given you the *armoire*, Bunny, if I'd known you wanted it, but you see I wasn't consulted."

"Neither did you know me," retorted Bunny, then stood fingering the *armoire* reflectively.

"I always admired it," she said, "And when the things were sold, well, as you said—a friend bought it for me."

"I wonder why the other one was left," Sabina said. "Now I know the furniture is really mine I shall keep it there until—until I have somewhere to put it myself."

"Did your aunt not make over the money to you?" Bunny asked sharply, and Sabina answered as she had replied to Brock.

"I expect she thought it would help with my keep."

Bunny sniffed but said no more, and soon she was in the middle of an orgy of dusting which left little margin for conversation.

The next day Sabina was conscious of change as soon as she got up. Willie Washer wore a new jersey and was tending the garden with unusual zest, and Mrs. Cheadle had arrived for once in time to get the breakfast. Even the house had about it an elusive impression of difference, Sabina thought, but perhaps it was the morning's post which was really responsible. Certainly both Brock and Bunny received letters which caused them to frown, while for Sabina had come one of the rare postcards from France.

"Tante says that she has now concluded arrangements with M. Bergerac and I may expect them soon," she announced, not yet quite believing in the end of the fairy-tale.

"Does she put that on a postcard?" asked Bunny with a frown of distaste.

"Oh, Tante never writes letters—at least to me," Sabina replied, and Brock, who had been paying no attention, remarked:

"I shall have to return—at least for a time."

"Is your letter from Madame Jouvez?" Bunny inquired, showing no surprise.

"No," he replied, frowning.

"Well, mine is. She is in England and wishes to know if you are staying here. She tried the old address and was given mine."

"Jeanne Jouvez?' Well, I've been expecting to hear."

"Do you want me to reply?"

"Yes—no, I'll write myself. You wouldn't care for her to invade your prim rectory, Bunny. Jeanne is very feminine and a little exacting. She wouldn't fit with your routine."

But he did not speak of the unknown Madame Jouvez as if news of her displeased him, thought Sabina, trying not to appear to be listening. They had clearly forgotten her.

"As you wish," said Bunny a little coldly. "But if you are going away—"

"I'm going where she can easily find me," he said, and Sabina felt a small chill creep round her heart!

"I, too, will have to go soon," she said clearly. "I don't think you were listening, Brock, but I have heard from Tante that she has settled everything with M. Bergerac and I may expect them soon."

"Really?" he said politely. "Well, that must please you,

Sabina. M. Bergerac's intentions have been none too clear to date, have they?"

She flushed at his tone and Bunny said:

"That was not kind, Brock. It is you who have put doubts in the child's mind, if she has any. I have understood lately that if Sabina is willing to marry a man she has not met, there is no objection on his part."

Sabina's knuckles showed suddenly white as she clenched her fists on the breakfast table.

"And supposing I'm not," she cried unexpectedly. "Supposing I decide to work for my living and then marry someone of my own choice, whether he has any money or not! I could let the house to cold-blooded M. Bergerac if that's all he really wants, couldn't I?"

"Well, now," said Brock with interest, "that *is* an idea!"

"You're upset, dear child," Bunny said, recognising hysteria when she saw it. "I should go and lie down, if I were you."

"Of course I'm upset!" shouted Sabina, thumping on the table. "I'm sick and tired of the name of Bergerac and I never want to see him as long as I live! I won't lie down, either—I shall go out on the moor and fall in a bog and drown."

She pushed back her chair with such violence that it crashed to the floor, and ran out of the room, her shoulders shaking with sobs.

"She probably will, too," said Brock, getting to his feet. "Dear me, scenes so early in the morning! Still, it's heartening to see the worm turn at last, isn't it, Bunny?"

But Bunny looked distresesd.

"It may be heartening for you, having achieved what you set out to do, but I don't like any of this—I don't like it at all," she said.

Brock, looking out of the window, paid little attention.

"There she goes," he said, "and without a coat, too, the little fool! Why it always has to be me to go after her when she runs away, I don't know."

He left the room with his stiff, dragging gait, and snatching up a coat from the hall-stand, went out of the house. Willie, his mouth hanging open with surprise, leant on his hoe and watched.

* * *

Sabina ran, the March wind stinging her ears. Over the gravestones and rickety wall she sprang, careless of footholds, and as once before, she took a direct line over the moor, ignoring paths and sheep tracks. She was running away, this time not only from René Bergerac and his complacent plans, but from Bunny's disapproval and Brock's heartless mockery.

She heard him behind her, shouting, and ran faster, her skirt tearing on gorse and thorn bush, her stockings slashed and the tender skin beneath. He would not catch her with that stiff leg of his, and it gave her an empty but wild sense of satisfaction to know that he must suffer for his pursuit of her.

Brock kept the flashing scarlet jersey in sight, but she ran too fast for him and he cursed the crippling infirmity which held him back, the coat he carried hampering his movements. She was heading for the bog into which she had childishly threatened to fall and drown, and he shouted again. But it was not the bog that Sabina fell into, indeed she scarcely recognised the smooth and lovely patch of brilliant emerald for what it was. A loose boulder slipped beneath her flying feet and she was thrown down into a clump of bracken which hid the stony bed of a little stream.

The breath was knocked out of her and she lay there gasping and sobbing while the chilly water soaked into her shoes. When Brock caught up with her she was trying to rise and blood was trickling from a little cut on the rounded forehead.

"Well!" he observed, looking down at her grimly. "See what you get for running away."

She did not answer or look up, and flinging the coat in the bracken he knelt awkwardly beside her, his stiff leg at a painful angle.

"Are you hurt?" he asked and ran his fingers over her slender bones.

"Of course I'm hurt," she gasped, "I think I've broken all my b-bones."

He was breathing heavily himself, for the sudden exertion had been great and he was out of training for such a spurt over rough ground.

"Not you," he said. "You're winded, that's all. Stay quiet till you get your breath back."

He spoke roughly but his hands were tender as he dipped his handkerchief in the stream and bathed the cut on her forehead. He took off her shoes and laddered stockings and washed the scratches on her legs, then lifted her gently onto her feet. She was still crying and every so often she drew a deep, painful breath.

"What goaded you so abruptly?" he asked with sudden gentleness. "Was it your aunt's postcard or my regrettable teasing, or a bit of both?"

"Teasing!" she cried. "Do you call it that?"

But the dark face was no longer forbidding, and as he shifted his position in the bracken she knew that his leg was troubling him.

"Oh, Brock . . ." she said and bowed her head against his breast, weeping afresh.

His arms closed round her and he held her close, supporting the light weight of her body while his cheek brushed her hair.

"Poor child . . ." he said. "Poor little driven lamb . . ."

She heard only the stream chattering over stones, and the harsh, hard breathing beneath her head. The March wind swept over scrub and heather, buffeting them gently, but it was a kindly wind and spring was under their feet and in the distant bleating of lambs across the moor.

"Come," he said. "Come and sit down for awhile before we start home."

There was a small sheltered hollow in the boulders close by, and he lifted her over the stream and the rough stones which would have been harsh to bare feet. He picked up the coat and wrapped it round her and they sat together, their backs against a flat boulder, the thin sunshine warm on their faces.

"You haven't answered my question," he said. "What made you run out of the house like that?"

Her head on the slender, childish neck drooped against his shoulder.

"I think it was because you were going away—to Madame Jouvez," she said.

He smiled above her head.

"But if you thought that, why should it matter if you married René Bergerac?"

"I don't know," she said and sighed. "But the two were connected in my mind. You see—until I met you I had no knowledge of men. Tante's arrangements seemed natural, for I had grown up with them, but now—"

"Now," said Brock with an indulgence that had a bitter tinge, "the first man you meet can show you you are a woman and not a child."

"Yes," she said, "but for you that wasn't so. For you I have just been a child to tease and not take seriously."

"Do you think so? Can't you understand that under the teasing I've been concerned for your ignorance?"

"Possibly," she answered with grave politeness, "but it was hardly your affair, was it?"

"Well, perhaps more than you think," he said. "I know the Bergerac family, you forget."

"I don't forget," she replied. "But you've never given me a picture of René Bergerac that means a thing. He might be fat, but he is not like a head waiter; he is famous but not attractive, and he has poor health of which nobody seems to know the cause."

"True, not an encouraging portrait," he said. "And what now?"

"Now?"

"Well, you announced at breakfast that you aren't prepared to marry a man you have never met—that you would work and marry the man of your choice, whether he had any money or not. Do you still feel that way?"

"Yes," she said. "I know now that what you once said to me is true. You shouldn't go into marriage expecting the worst. I didn't, of course, expect anything—I'd never thought much about such things, but now—"

"And what's made you grow up?"

But she was not prepared to reveal all her growing pains to Brock, so gentle in this hour of crisis, so careless of what he took and what he gave.

"Different things, I suppose," she answered evasively. "When will you be going, Brock?"

"Probably tomorrow."

Her forehead creased in pain.

"So soon? When you come back I will have gone, too."

He slipped an arm round her shoulders.

"No, you won't," he said. "I shall be gone a week, not more. When I come back——"

"Yes? When you come back?"

His fingers tightened suddenly on her shoulder, and he swung her abruptly round into the circle of his arms.

"When I come back would you marry me—or don't I qualify for the man of your choice, with or without money?" he asked surprisingly.

She looked up into his dark face and knew him for a stranger still. She had no defence against him, but what should he want of her, this man who loved the mountains, cheated by nature of his rightful heritage?

"Well?" he said. "Do I offer no more attractive alternative to the elderly M. Bergerac?"

"Oh, don't," she said, shutting her eyes, "don't joke about him, now."

"I'm sorry," he said, "I wasn't joking. I had thought that for me you had developed a small fondness that was a better starting point than that other, but I wasn't sure. Open your eyes, Sabina, and tell me if you think you could be happy with me."

Her lashes fluttered in the two little crescents which gave such innocence to her face, and her mouth curved tremulously into another.

"Yes, I could be happy with you," she said and sighed, for what, after all, was happiness? If one person could love enough, she thought, that perhaps would do.

"Then look at me."

She opened her eyes and saw his face, lean, hard and dominant, but with a fleeting tenderness about the twisted mouth which filled the empty places of her heart. She slipped her arms about his neck drawing herself closer to him, and lifted her tired face for his kiss.

"Am I engaged to you now?" she asked, still uncertain as to whether she had been proposed to or not.

"No," he said. "You can't be, as the good Marthe would have it, promised to two men at once."

"But that other—I'm still waiting to hear from René Bergerac."

"I daresay, but we'll take one thing at a time. You will write to your aunt?"

It was more a statement than a question.

"Yes," she replied. "But it won't be easy, Brock. I'm under age and Tante has set her heart on this marriage."

"But you are prepared to fight?"

"If it will do any good, but you don't know Tante. I have never been able to stand up to her about anything that mattered."

"Well, she can't force you to marry against your will."

"No, but—Brock, could we not—elope—before she returns from France?"

The old-fashioned expression sounded prim and rather absurd and he gave her hair a tweek.

"Running away is your solution for everything, isn't it?" he said. "Eventually, I shall see your aunt myself, but in the meantime you must write yourself, and I think to Bergerac too."

"To René? But we have never communicated."

"I daresay, but from what we can gather now, the deal has been completed. Don't you think you owe him an explanation?"

"I suppose so. Do you think—if I suggest letting him Penruthan for a nominal sum, he would be content?"

He shrugged.

"Who knows? The place needs a packet spending on it before it's habitable as a hotel, and he may not feel the expense is justified for a property he doesn't own, besides—he may have fallen for that glamorous photograph and your aunt's glowing descriptions."

The old mockery was back in his voice and she said unhappily:

"It must all sound a joke to you, but I wish—I wish I could have returned Penruthan to the Bergeracs all the same. It belongs in the family."

"It belongs to the English branch," he said. "It was the property of René Bergerac's wife to do with as she pleased."

"Yet he married her for it, just as the present Bergerac would marry me."

"And that, for all you know, may be another of your aunt's little fabrications," he said shortly. "Mary Bergerac was a beautiful woman. Old René, I think, was a fool. He played around with women of no consequence until it was too late to mend his broken marriage—but that, as your aunt seems fond of telling you, is the French way."

Sabina was silent, remembering. Tante, too, had been one of those women of no consequence, and, if she was to be believed, the final cause of the separation.

He seemed to sense an unwillingness in her to agree and said with a certain harshness:

"You owe nothing to Lucille Faivre, my dear. She adopted you for what she could get out of the arrangement, cheated you of money that was rightfully yours on the sale of the furniture, and is now prepared to barter you to a stranger of doubtful reputation for her own ends. Wake up, Sabina! If the old loyalties are too strong, or you too weak to resist, then say so now and I'll leave you alone."

She coloured hotly at his words, but she suddenly sat up straight against his shoulder and her eyes were clear and steady.

"You're right, of course, and perhaps I've always known it," she said. "I'm not weak, Brock, once I understand. I've just not been allowed to grow up."

He took her face between his hands and kissed her with tenderness.

"Forgive me if I seem rough with you sometimes, child," he said. "You must teach me tolerance."

Her lips this time remained passive under his while she wondered if there was anything she might teach him, whether tolerance of an untutored mind, or the love which he had not declared in so many words.

"Bunny will tell you I've taken an unfair advantage," he said, impatient at her silence. "Are you ready to help me bridge the years between us and not resent what I've been?"

"I don't know what you've been, Brock. I only know I love you," she said.

"Bless you for that!" he murmured and stooped to put on her shoes for her, saying they must be getting back.

The coat he had brought was an old one of Bunny's and it reached to her ankles, making her look absurd and very young. He surveyed her, laughing, then tucked an arm through hers and turned for home.

"Madame Jouvez—is she part of the business to which you must attend?" Sabina asked once.

"Very likely, but you should be grateful I didn't allow her to come here. You and she wouldn't care about each other, I fancy," he replied with amusement. "Jeanne is a charming, determined young widow and knows exactly what she wants."

"A widow?"

"Yes—does that alarm you? Will you inquire about the ladies in my past if we marry, Sabina?"

"No," she said.

They walked in silence and Brock, who was limping badly, asked her as they reached the rectory what she had been thinking about.

"I was wondering if you really *can* cook that Spanish dish with the extraordinary name," she said with the inconsequence that could both delight and exasperate him.

"Arroz Paella alla Valenciana?" he laughed. "Yes, I really can. One day, my chicken, you shall have that cooking lesson you were so anxious for the other night. Now run upstairs and make yourself presentable before Bunny catches you. She wouldn't approve of bare legs in March or a torn skirt."

Sabina went slowly upstairs to her room and sat on the bed, staring at Brock's mountains. Kanchenjunga . . . Everest . . . and the cool peaks of the Alps . . . Could she compete with them, she wondered . . . could she fulfil a want so dimly understood? Had he not scooped her up carelessly because just now he needed her?

She sighed, then rested her cheek in the curve of her hand, smiling gratefully. Was it not enough to have found sanctuary, to have found affection and that first miraculous stirring of the heart?

She lay down on the bed for a moment because a great lassitude had claimed her and was almost instantly asleep.

CHAPTER EIGHT

WHEN she came downstairs for luncheon she felt shy at sitting down again with Brock and Bunny after the events of the morning, but both of them were as usual. If Brock had already spoken to Bunny she gave no sign of being the recipient of romantic confidences and Brock himself seemed preoccupied with his coming departure.

Sabina knew an unreasoning disappointment, and as the day went on she began to wonder if she had imagined the whole thing. Only when Brock asked her with abrupt reminder if she had written her letters was she brought back to reality, but he looked impatient when she answered in the negative and told her sharply that she had better do so at once.

"Unless," he said, "you've thought better of it and are reluctant to give up the comforts of the Château Berger, after all."

"No," she replied, ignoring the mockery, "but I thought —well, perhaps I was beginning to think you hadn't been serious."

"Because I didn't lead you home to Bunny in triumphant glory? There's time enough for that when other matters are settled."

"Yes—yes, I see."

"You don't see at all, my poor innocent," he said, ruffling her hair. "Perhaps you should meet the egregious M. Bergerac before deciding. He might have charms for you, after all, and certainly he has riches."

"Tante was the one who wanted riches, not me," Sabina said, wishing he would stop talking in this vein now that he knew how she felt about him.

"She won't be as unworldly as you are, my dear," he retorted. "You don't know anything about me, or even what I do for a living."

"You've never told me. What do you do for a living?"

"That can wait," he said with his old arrogance. "Run along and write those letters."

She did so dutifully, sitting at Bunny's little *escritoire* and sucking her pen like an ill-prepared schoolgirl. It was difficult to compose a suitable epistle to a man one had never met and who had not, to all intents and purposes, made a formal offer of marriage.

"What shall I say?" she asked Brock, who was selecting books for the journey from Bunny's shelves.

"What? Oh, just say 'Dear Sir, I must regretfully decline the honour you may be thinking of doing me in the matter of marriage. Yours truly . . .' "

She laughed, but, as once before, she wanted to hit him, too. It was unfair and unkind to put all the onus on her, she thought, and made a large blot on the clean paper and had to start again.

At last the letters were written and Willie Washer took them to the post on his way home. Sabina saw Brock regarding her with a lifted eyebrow.

"Are you experiencing those well-known doubts at having burnt your boats?" he asked.

She got up from the desk, stretching her arms above her head to ease her aching back.

"No," she said. "The doubts will probably come with Tante's reply."

He laughed, but not unkindly.

"I think this must be the first time you've made a major decision for yourself," he said.

"No," she said again. "The first time was when I ran away and left my purse and luggage in the train."

"So it was. The whole thing looks like fate—or Providence, as Bunny would say."

"Brock—" She stood with her back to him, fingering the *armoire*, and watching the fitful reflection of firelight in its polished surface, "why do you want to marry me?"

"Why do you suppose?"

"Well, it could be that you, like M. Bergerac, need a wife, or it could be just wanting something that's promised to someone else."

"You haven't a very flattering opinion of the two men in your life, have you?"

"I don't know René Bergerac and I don't understand you," she said, and suddenly felt his hands on her shoulders.

"In other words, you're finding me an unsatisfactory sort of lover, aren't you?" he said.

A lover . . . strangely enough she had never thought of him as that, but as he drew her head back against his breast she knew that was what she wanted him to be.

"When I come back, we'll talk of such things," he said. "Till then have faith and patience and go on loving me if you will, for that will warm me."

It was a curious thing to say, she thought, and remembered that the business which was taking him away had something to do with Madame Jouvez.

"Have you, too, to become—disentangled?" she asked.

She could not see his face but thought he smiled above her head.

"If you're thinking of Jeanne, the part she has played in my life carries no ties," he said ambiguously. "Perhaps I want to bid my old love farewell."

"The mountains—you are going to the mountains?" she said, and then wondered if after all he was perhaps speaking of Jeanne Jouvez.

"Perhaps," he said and dropped a light kiss on the top of her head. "Stop speculating, my child; your guesses are probably all wrong."

"I'm not really curious," she said, and he let her go.

"No," he said with tenderness, "you're the most incurious young woman it's ever been my fortune to meet. Perhaps that's half your charm."

She turned to him swiftly, but Bunny was bringing in the tea-tray and in a moment the afternoon was just like any other with the three of them making casual conversation while the lamplight reflected in the late vicar's ugly Victorian silver. Too soon it was supper-time, and afterwards Sabina helped Bunny wash up while Brock went upstairs to pack.

"You look tired, my dear," Bunny said when they had finished. "I should go early to bed after your adventures of the morning."

It was the first reference she had made to the day's unexpected happenings, and even now she might only be alluding to Sabina's cut forehead and scratched legs.

"Not yet," Sabina said, listening for sounds of Brock's return from upstairs, but Bunny was used to nursery procrastination and only replied with a smile:

138

"It would be advisable if you want to be up early to-morrow to say good-bye to Brock."

Obediently Sabina went. She hoped she might meet Brock on the stairs and be kissed good night, but only her own shadow marched solitary before her in the light of her candle, and although she called good night as she passed his door, he could not have heard, for he made no answer.

She wakened early and was reminded of the morning the robin had died as she dressed quickly in the chill half-light, but hurry though she did, there was little time for more than the fleeting impressions of departure; the village taxi at the door, Bunny hovering in the cold hall with last-minute reminders of articles which might have been forgotten in the packing, and Brock in a dark lounge suit which Sabina had not seen before.

"Look after the child," he said as he kissed Bunny goodbye, but Sabina he did not kiss, and under the watching eyes of Bunny and the taxi-driver, she did not care to make the first advances.

"Good-bye," she said; "give my love to the mountains."

He was unfamiliar in his well-tailored clothes and although he smiled at her he was a stranger again.

"*Au revoir*," he replied. "Good-bye has a final sound. No running away before I get back, mind, Sabina. Next time you will be punished."

She watched him limp to the taxi and get in, and the next minute he was gone; to that destination of which she had no knowledge, to the mountains, perhaps; perhaps to Jeanne Jouvez.

"Shut the door, dear," said Bunny prosaically. "These early mornings are very chilly still, and the house gets cold quickly before the fires are lighted."

"It's like the morning the robin died," Sabina said, shutting the door, and Bunny smiled.

"That," she replied with prim reproof, "is an exaggeration. There is no snow and Brock has not met with any mishap. He is merely catching a train."

Sabina laughed and gave her a quick hug.

"Dear Bunny," she said affectionately, "you have a wonderful gift for reducing things to their proper level.

Let me light the fires for you. Mrs. Cheadle's sure to be late again."

"Well, perhaps just the parlour fire to warm it up for breakfast," Bunny said. "As we are all down early I shall take the opportunity to have a thorough spring-clean of the bedrooms. You shall help me."

*   *   *

Sabina did plenty of helping the next few days. Bunny, she supposed, held the old idea that busy hands curbed wandering thoughts, but sometimes she longed to sit idle and dream or walk on the moor with just her reflections for company. Even out of doors a mild routine was set for her, and she helped Willie in the garden or accompanied Bunny on her self-imposed rounds to her husband's old parishioners.

"Of course, Mrs. Weymouth, the new rector's wife, has first call in these matters and I have to be careful not to tread on her toes, but the old people like to be remembered," Bunny would say, and Sabina had her first taste of the parochial life which had been kept well in the background during Brock's visit.

Mrs. Weymouth, it soon became apparent, did not take kindly to Bunny's gentle interference and probably despised her. The Reverend Cyril was not a Cornishman and, explained Bunny, less in harmony with the village than her late husband. There were the ever-recurring problems of poor Willie Washer's fitness to look after the graves, and Mrs. Cheadle's preference for working at the old rectory rather than the new one. Sabina became soothed by the small, unimportant saga as she was with Willie's undemanding company in the garden.

Often he was morose and seemed to blanket what intelligence he had with a deliberate stupidity, but sometimes he was gay, remembering old rhymes and capering joyously while he chanted them. Sabina was often surprised by the strange odds and ends of knowledge he possessed. She liked to sit on an upturned wheelbarrow while Willie pounded the hard, unbroken soil with his hoe, saying:

> *Come, butter, come.*
> *Come, butter, come.*
> *Peter stands at the gate*
> *Waiting for a buttered cake.*
> *Come, butter, come!*

" 'Tes a churning rhyme," he explained when she asked him. "My grandma used to make proper butter."

"Do you remember your grandmother, Willie?" she asked, but his face immediately clouded.

"Nay. My auntie's all I've ever knowd. Mebbe I'm a foundling," he answered vaguely, and Sabina thought of that other unkind little rhyme made up by the jeering village children.

"No," she said gently. "You're kind Willie Washer who knows a lot more than those silly children in the village."

"That's right," he said cheerfully and smiled at her with great sweetness. "You'm a proper little maid, yourself, missy."

He suddenly sprang in the air and chanted hoarsely:

> *Underneath this hazelin mote.*
> *There's a braggarty worm with speckled throat;*
> *Nine double is he . . .*

" 'Tes for snakebite, see? They be adders up on t'moor. You be careful, missy."

"Oh, I will. How does it go on?"

"I forget," he said, suddenly losing interest. It was usually the same. The curious couplets sounded even stranger recited in his broad Cornish accent, and so often they broke off temptingly, leaving Sabina tantalised and eager for more.

Sometimes she taught him the rhymes she remembered herself from the days when curious spells and jingles were all she had to while away the hours when she was left alone in a hotel bedroom and told not to make a noise. He liked best the rhymes which depended on numbers, like his own charm against snakebite. *The twelve Days of Christmas* delighted him and Sabina's own favourite which began with the twelve apostles and finished with the one left all alone, but he could never memorise them and she often wondered why his simple mind should have retained the half-remembered verses of his own.

Discussing him with Bunny she was touched by the older woman's concern for the boy.

"I worry about him, sometimes," she said. "The present rector has been saying for a long time that he should be put away."

"Oh, but why?" exclaimed Sabina indignantly. "He's only simple, and that's quite different, surely. Willie wouldn't hurt a fly. The only time he gets violent is if he hears that hateful jingle."

"He's safe enough so far," Bunny replied with reserve, "but there's nobody really to look after him. That old aunt he lives with is a slatternly lazy woman and that dark little shop of hers is no place for a feeble-minded boy."

"But you wouldn't—" began Sabina, her clear, wide-spaced eyes stretched with disbelief, and Bunny touched the young face affectionately.

"No, of course not, dear. It's not in my power for one thing, although Mr. Weymouth could make the necessary arrangements if he wished."

"And he does wish, the hateful man! I think he's just like Willie's braggarty worm!"

"Hush, dear; that is needlessly extravagant," Bunny reproved. "The rector, after all, must do the best he can for his parishioners, whether they are good, or evil-doers, or just naturals, like poor Willie."

"Naturals?"

"It's a country word and so kindly, I always think, for however we are born we are God's creatures."

"Yes . . ." said Sabina slowly. "And there's a pattern, isn't there? There must be a pattern."

"Of course. You'll find yours."

"Me?"

"Well, wasn't that what you were thinking of? Brock will find his too—in fact I think he's found it."

"Oh!" Sabina said, her lowered lashes forming crescents of withdrawal. "I always think Brock's pattern is complete. He knows what he wants, and others must conform."

Bunny looked at her with the same kindly tolerance she showed to Willie.

"Do you think so?" she said. "But you have so much

142

to learn yet, my dear. No pattern is complete until—"

"Until what?"

"Well, perhaps none of us really know. But don't be misled, Sabina. Brock is a great deal older than you and has led a very different life. I have always thought that he has missed the simple things. You may be an essential part of the pattern."

"Do you really think so?"

"Naturally. Why else, do you suppose, does he want to marry you?"

"I don't know," Sabina said doubtfully. "M. Bergerac, after all, would have married me for a house."

Bunny looked suddenly a little tired.

"Yes," she said, "but that need not concern you now, need it? In a little while everything will be clearer."

"Clearer?" To Sabina it was a foolish remark. Brock had made things clear in one respect before he left, but there was so much to doubt, now that he had gone, so many facets that were not clear at all.

Bunny sighed.

"I've always hoped—" she began, then thought better of what she had been going to say. "Don't puzzle your head with needless matters now. Brock will be back very soon, and if in the meantime time hangs heavily, go and play with Willie. You are good for him, I think, because you are young. You should take it as a compliment, Sabina. He doesn't say his rhymes to everyone."

Sabina was grateful that someone should afford her special consideration, even if it was only poor simple Willie Washer. There had been few times in her life when she had been the focus of attention, and since she had come to Truan she had discovered slowly that she might merit importance of a kind; to Willie, who accepted her as the playmate he had never had, to Bunny, because perhaps her heart had never grown away from the young she used to teach, and to Brock—well, for him it might be more complex. He wanted her, yes, but could she ever measure up to those half understood standards, or meet his demands with a maturity that would match his own?

The days went on and Sabina began to watch for the post, not for a letter from Brock, but for that expected angry reply from Tante.

"I do not think you will hear for a while," Bunny said, and Sabina was again conscious that both the governess and Brock had knowledge which she herself did not share.

"She's more likely to come herself to reason with me," she said ruefully, but Bunny shook her head.

"Bunny—" Sabina said impulsively, "you know more than you will tell me, don't you? Why are you always so sure of Tante's reactions?"

"I'm not sure," replied Bunny a little repressively, "and I know nothing that is my business to pass on. A governess learns very early not to betray a confidence or repeat gossip, if she wants to keep her job."

"But you aren't a governess any more, and I've always known the old gossip about Tante. She makes no secret of her affair with old Bergerac."

"Very likely. Lucille Faivre was always a vain woman, but these things were long ago and do not concern me now."

"Now! Then Tante hurt you at some time or other?"

"Only indirectly. We will not discuss Mrs. Lamb's affairs, or Brock's till he returns, dear child."

Sabina sighed. Bunny could be firm enough when she chose, and whatever her knowledge, she was clearly not prepared to share it.

Despite the many occupations with which Bunny filled her days, Sabina began to grow impatient. Brock was gone she knew not where and there was still no news from Tante. The days were mild and spring-like and carried an air of expectancy, whether of the approaching season or the dictates of her own blossoming spirit, she did not know, but she had a desire to visit Penruthan once more and wander again, for perhaps the last time, through the deserted rooms.

Bunny she knew, would not permit a walk across the moor after that first alarming experience and she went out to the garden to find Willie and try to persuade him to take her.

He was amongst the graves, as usual, and she saw him bend lovingly over a clump of primroses, his rough hair the same colour as the flowers. She sat on a tombstone and watched his clumsy fingers dealing so tenderly with

144

the choked roots of the plant, and he smiled at her over his shoulder and went on working in silence.

She was used to these silences of Willie's now. It was not one of his sullen days, and his face as he bent over the primroses was blank and childlike. Around them the graves lay, quiet and peaceful in the pale sunshine, and Sabina had come to understand the boy's strange liking for the churchyard.

"Willie," she said softly, "will you do something for me?"

"Mebbe," he replied with his usual caution.

"Will you show me the way over the moor to Penruthan?"

He sat back on his heels in the grass and shook his head violently.

"Nay," he said as once before; "I'll not go there. 'Tes 'aunted."

"Nonsense!" Sabina reproved. "It's just a great old empty house, but there are no ghosts."

" 'Tes 'aunted," he repeated, and she regarded him thoughtfully, her head on one side.

"And if it were," she said. "I'm surprised at you, Willie, being afraid of a poor ghost when you'll spend all day in the graveyard."

"The daid don't 'aunt—they lies quiet," he said stubbornly. "I likes they daid 'uns—they'm powerful kind."

"Poor Willie," she said gently; "aren't people kind to you?"

His mild eyes clouded for a moment.

"Mis' Fennell and Maister Brock be kind, and you too, missy—you'm a proper little maid."

"Then you wouldn't like me to get lost, like I did before, would you?" she coaxed, but he suddenly jumped to his feet, flapping his arms at a flock of starlings which had swooped on the churchyard.

"Git away, git away, you noisy varmints!" he cried and Sabina was reminded of the garden boy in *Prunella* chanting:

> Oh, you naughty birds, now, will you
> Come into my garden and I'll kill you . . .

"Don't you like birds?" she asked.

"Nay, they'm always chittering. This be a place for quiet—quiet and sleep."

She remembered Brock saying once that there was a natural poetry in the feeble-minded and she remembered his gentleness when he spoke to the boy and the patience that was no foreign to his nature.

"You're fond of Mr. Brock, aren't you?" she said, wanting to talk about him even to someone who was simple.

"He be gone abroad now," he said sadly.

"Abroad?" Then she remembered that this was only another west-country expression not to be taken literally.

"But he's coming back very soon."

Willie dropped on his knees again, still shaking his head.

"Next year mebbe, but 'tes no manner of use," he said.

"No, soon—at the end of the week, very likely. Perhaps he'll bring you a present, Willie."

He gave a slow grin at that, for presents were an unfailing delight to Willie.

"If you show me the way to Penruthan, I'll give you a present, too," Sabina said quickly.

"What'll 'e be?"

"You shall choose. My aunt sent Mrs. Fennell some money for me last week. You shall have whatever you like."

She anxiously watched the struggle in his face. It had now become absurdly important to her to visit Penruthan, and if Willie would not take her she must go the long weary way by the road.

"I'll show 'e the way, then," he said suddenly, "because you'm kind to poor Willie, but I'll not set foot in the house, mind. I'll come no nearer than gate in wall."

"Oh, thank you!" she cried gratefully. "I'll go and ask Mrs. Fennell if she will spare you."

Bunny was not enthusiastic, but if Willie Washer had consented to go as well, she said, she would have no objection.

"But follow him, and don't be tempted to choose your own path," she warned. "Willie may be simple but he knows every inch of the moor and you'll come to no harm with him."

146

They set off after an early luncheon. Willie shambled ahead, sure-footed as any of the moorland ponies, for all his ungainliness, and Sabina followed, the light breeze sweet on her face, while the early springtide drew forth fresh beauty from the moor. Now they were crossing the stream into which she had fallen on the day she had run away from Brock, and there were the hollowed boulders where they had sat and he had asked her to marry him. How life had changed for her since she had come to Truan, she thought, and laughed aloud as she remembered her fear of him that night of their first strange meeting.

Hearing her, Willie laughed too, the gentle, vacant laugh of a child who does not know why it is happy, and presently he began to sing in a queer cracked voice which had a certain sweetness, and Sabina joined in, humming a melody she thought she recognised. It was a strange, lightheaded passage across the moor. Presently the high walls of Penruthan rose to meet them over the next rise and Willie drew back.

"Be 'e going in?" he asked, still doubting her folly, and she laughed.

"Of course. You wait here, Willie. I'll give a shout when I'm ready to go back."

She left him standing there, and pushed open the broken door in the wall, remembering that snowy night when she had come upon it unawares. Now she could see the neglect into which the place had fallen. A wilderness of vegetation lay before her, and the house itself, without its concealing shroud of snow, spoke mutely of decay and the long neglect of years.

Only when she reached the terrace did Sabina remember that she had forgotten the key. Brock had given her a key that other time, but she did not think now he could have got it from the agent, whose office was in Truro or Bodmin. Brock then, or Bunny, must have had a key of their own, and that in itself was puzzling.

She walked round the house looking for a door or window that might be open, but the shutters were firmly bolted and no door yielded to her touch. She went round to the front of the house, nearly crying with vexation, and stopped suddenly. A small car stood on the overgrown

147

drive and the great front door was wide open. For a moment she thought Brock had returned unexpectedly, but the car was not his, and after a moment's hesitation Sabina went into the house and called.

It was eerie standing in that vaulted hall with her voice echoing back from the roof high above her. No one answered, and she began to walk through the chain of rooms looking for the intruder, but there was no sign of a living soul. She thought of Willie's fear of ghosts, then laughed a little uncertainly; ghosts did not arrive in cars. Sabina knew a moment's panic. In this great house no one would hear if you called; any minute the front door might slam behind the unknown visitor and she would be locked in for the night. She turned with a feeling of stricture in her throat and ran swiftly back through the empty rooms to the hall. The front door was still open and a woman was coming very slowly down the stone staircase.

Sabina stood and watched her. She walked with graceful deliberation, as though she was making a studied entrance down a flight of stage stairs. She was bareheaded and her red hair was caught like a flaming aureole as she passed through a slanting ray of light. There was something very strange in the progress of that slow descent, for although she could not know that she was being observed, she gave an impression of being watched by a large audience.

"Who are you?" asked Sabina, speaking suddenly and loudly as she came forward out of the shadows.

The woman paused, but did not start, and her long, slender hand caressed the stone carving of the blaustrade.

"Who are *you*?" she retorted, and her voice was deep and husky with the faintest trace of a foreign accent. She completed her passage down the stairs and smiled as she saw Sabina more clearly. Her mouth was exquisitely painted and her long eyes shadowed with mascara.

"Oh, just a little girl," she said with amusement. "Do you trespass, finding the door open?"

"I found the door open, yes, but I wasn't trespassing," Sabina said. "What are *you* doing here?"

"I have an order to view. This is quite correct, you know."

"The house is not for sale. Didn't they tell you that?"

"Oh, yes, but I had a fancy to see the place that a good friend of mine is willing to barter his heart and his freedom for. It does not impress me."

Sabina knew a moment's excitement.

"Are you a friend of the Bergeracs, then?" she asked, and saw the other woman's fine eyebrows lift in surprise.

"Why, yes; but how should you know?" she replied, then her eyes suddenly narrowed. "It is not possible that you are the litle English girl who hopes to marry René!" She threw back her head and laughed till the house echoed.

"You are not very polite," said Sabina gravely. "I'm the owner of the house, yes."

The woman descended the remaining stairs and her high heels rang sharply on the stone. She was taller than Sabina and very elegant.

"You are Mademoiselle Lamb?" she said, her eyes travelling with amusement over the girl.

"Yes," said Sabina, very conscious of her rough skirt and jersey and the artless disorder of her hair. "And you?"

"I am Jeanne Jouvez. You have heard of me, perhaps?"

Sabina's eyes were guarded.

"Yes, but not from M. Bergerac," she said.

The woman's smile showed little even teeth, sharp as any cat's.

"No, no, it would be from Blaireau you have heard, of course," she said.

"Blaireau?" The name sounded strange.

"It is my nickname for the good Brock. Do you not know that *blaireau* is French for a badger? When I wish to tease I call him that."

"I see. But I understood that he had gone to see you. Why are you here?" asked Sabina, puzzled by yet another mysterious link with the Château Berger.

"But I told you, mademoiselle—to see for myself the house which is of such interest to my old friend, René Bergerac. And, look you, I find the bride elect also, so my curiosity is doubly rewarded," said Jeanne Jouvez. "Come, mademoiselle, let us walk through the rooms together and plan the future of this house, yes?" She put a hand lightly under Sabina's elbow and began to walk towards the first big salon.

Sabina was puzzled. Was it Brock or René Bergerac who held this woman's affections, if, indeed, she had affection to offer? Brock had said that the part she had played in his life carried no ties, but he had wished to keep Madame Jouvez from coming to Truan all the same.

"Now this," Jeanne was saying, "would make an excellent ballroom, no doubt, and the smaller salons have an air, yes; but the house is *triste*. I would not care to live here."

"You will not have to, madame," said Sabina politely. "If Penruthan became a hotel it would be the choice of guests whether they stayed or not."

Jeanne gave her a quick glance, as though she had underestimated an adversary, and Sabina knew in that moment that, she was, in fact, just that. Madame Jouvez, she thought, had more at stake than the doubtful future of an English country house.

"But not, *ma petite*, a choice for the wife of the proprietor," Jeanne said.

"But I—" began Sabina, then the other woman's meaning became suddenly plain.

Tante's hints, Marthe's philosophic conclusions were explained. The Bergeracs, both father and son, were given to entanglements of the heart. It was not surprising that René Bergerac might have committed himself more deeply with this elegant, utterly feminine woman before the need for a prudent marriage had arisen.

"Were you engaged to M. Bergerac?" she asked blankly.

"No. René has not thought of marriage until lately. And you, my little one—does the French arrangement not shock your sentimental English heart?" Jeanne sounded amused.

"I'm not easily shocked by a business arrangement," said Sabina, wishing to hold on to her advantage a little longer. "I have a French aunt."

"Ah, yes, Lucille Lamb."

"You have met her?"

"Naturally. I have been staying until a week past at the Château Berger."

The colour came into Sabina's cheeks. She could not like or trust this woman, who would, she felt instinctively, have little compassion where another woman was concerned, but she knew Tante. She knew that Tante, more ruthless still, would have allowed no one to stand in her way when she held the trump card.

"Forgive me, madame," she said awkwardly, "but if you—if you want René Bergerac for yourself, I—I'm not standing in the way."

Jeanne leaned against the dusty *armoire* that was the pair to Bunny's, and surveyed Sabina with insolent amusement.

"And Lucille Faivre has already taught you that?" she said.

"What?" asked Sabina stupidly.

"That though you shall *ranger* yourself to the best advantage you will do well to close your eyes to the women your husband finds necessary to him?"

Now the bright colour mounted high to Sabina's cheekbones. Jeanne made her feel gauche and immature, but she stood her ground.

"No, I didn't mean that," she said. "I meant that you and René Bergerac are free to follow whatever plans you may have had, because I am not going to marry him. You would have left before my letters arrived at the Château."

It was strange, talking of such things in this empty house, she thought uneasily; when you stopped speaking a silence fell, as if your voice had been an affront to the deserted rooms. Jeanne looked at her lazily through narrowed lids. It was as if her news had made no impression.

"And you, perhaps, have had a girlish fancy for another—for Blaireau, the good badger who visits so dutifully his old governess?" Jeanne said.

"Do you want them both?" demanded Sabina, outraged, and Jeanne laughed.

"Perhaps," she said. "And what would you do then, my prim little schoolgirl?"

"I would hope," said Sabina steadily, "that I was—important enough to fight for."

"But no," said Jeanne, her eyes tilting at the corners with careless amusement; "it would be you who fight, my inexperienced child. Do you think you have much chance against a woman of the world?"

"My chances," said Sabina, lifting her chin, "would not depend on that, I hope. If a man wants a woman, I think he will know his own mind."

The other woman surveyed her, still with that indolent air of amusement, but her red, painted mouth twisted in a wry smile.

"No man knows his own mind when it comes to women," she said. "It is we, the desired, the pursued, who set the pace. That you must learn, *chérie*, before you can hope to hold your man."

For a moment Sabina knew uncertainty. Had not Brock said the day before he left that possibly he wished to bid farewell to his old love? Had he known of that *affaire* in this double game of intrigue?
with René Bergerac? Had she herself only been a catspaw

"I think, madame," she said, suddenly weary, "that we do no good here talking in riddles. I have told you that so far as M. Bergerac is concerned, I am no longer in the way."

"And Blaireau?"

But she did not know what Jeanne Jouvez had been to Brock nor how either linked up with the Château Berger.

"I think you have seen Brock in the last few days, haven't you?" she said, and Jeanne laughed.

"Oh, yes, but a man can talk nonsense, *hein*? Especially when he is unsure, himself."

"Very likely," said Sabina. "Have you finished your inspection, madame? We should be going, I think. The days are still short and I have some way to walk."

"And you do not care to leave me in possession, even though I have an order to view?" laughed Jeanne. "Well, let us go—this house has few attractions for me. May I drop you, mademoiselle, at the rectory if you have far to walk?"

"No, thank you," replied Sabina, remembering the waiting Willie. She did not ask where Jeanne was staying, nor if she knew when Brock would return.

Jeanne shrugged and began to walk back through the empty rooms, leaving a wave of heavy perfume behind her. In the hall she paused and tapped Sabina's cheek with cool, flippant fingers.

"We shall meet again, *chérie*," she said.

"I don't think so."

"But yes, for I am staying nearby and my business is not yet finished."

"That need not concern me," Sabina said, and Jeanne stepped on to the porch and stood laughing in the evening sunlight.

"You are a little fool!" she said with careless tolerance. "*Au revoir . . .*"

"Good-bye," replied Sabina, and slammed the door behind her.

She found Willie Washer where she had left him, sitting on a crumbling molehill beyond the wall. He seemed relieved to see her and, observing her disturbed face, remarked:

"Did 'e see a ghost, missy? You look like summat upset 'e."

"Not the kind you mean, Willie," she replied. "But perhaps you were right. It would have been better not to have gone to Penruthan."

"I told 'e so," he said with childlike satisfaction, and an odd, furtive look settled on his face as he set off across the moor with surprising speed.

Sabina looked back once. Penruthan lay grey and deserted beyond its broken walls; she would probably never see it again. As she followed Willie over the tracks and paths that only he could recognise, she thought longingly of Bunny and the quiet rectory, and of Brock's return.

CHAPTER NINE

"DID you know this Madame Jouvez who wrote to you for Brock's address?" Sabina asked Bunny that evening after supper.

Bunny was sorting embroidery silks on her knees by the fire and she looked up quickly, her pince-nez flashing in the light.

"No. Why do you ask?" she said.

"Because I met her today by chance at Penruthan. She had an order to view," Sabina said, and saw the mild alarm pinching Bunny's thin nostrils.

Sabina leant forward into the circle of light.

"Bunny," she said, "you and Brock have kept certain things from me, haven't you?"

Bunny went on sorting her silks. Blues here, pinks there, greens with yellow and neutral colours in a tidy pile of their own.

"What has Madame Jouvez been saying to you?" she asked.

"She talked in riddles, rather like Brock," she said; "but one thing seemed clear. She has an attachment for M. Bergerac and I—well, I'd rather interfered with her plans."

"She was rude to you?"

"Not exactly, but—well, she's very elegant and sophisticated. She plainly thought I was young and dowdy and inexperienced. She wasn't—very flattering about my chances in marriage."

"Marriage with whom?"

"With whom?" Sabina looked startled. "Oh, I see— but I told her that I was not going to marry M. Bergerac after all. I thought that would clear the air."

"And did it?"

Sabina considered, going over in her mind that unsatisfactory exchange with Jean Jouvez.

"I don't know," she said slowly. "She was rather strange altogether. I think she has also had a fondness for Brock."

"Very likely—and he for her." Bunny' voice was dry as she bent over her silks, and Sabina slipped to the floor by the governess's chair and laid her hands over the busy fingers.

"Bunny, you're keeping something from me," she said again. "Was Brock once fond of Madame Jouvez and did he finds out she was having an affair with René Bergerac? Is that the reason for all this—all this mystery?"

"Isn't it true Brock wishes to marry you, Sabina?"

"He said so."

"Then I hope you are not imagining that you have caught him on the rebound, whatever Madame Jouvez may have said to you."

Sabina flushed at the disapproval in Bunny's voice.

"No, I don't—I never thought about it," she said. "But—"

Bunny took off her pince-nez, which had made two little red marks either side of her nose, and looked into the young, uncertain face raised to hers.

"Keep these perplexities for Brock," she said gently. "He'll be back tomorow."

"Tomorrow!" There was a lilt in Sabina's voice and Bunny regarded her a little sadly.

"You're so young child," she said. "So ignorant of wordly matters. Don't get hurt if you find that life—and human relationships, perhaps—aren't as simple as you think."

"Are you warning me not to expect too much? I don't, you know," Sabina said, and her long throat looked young and tender in the firelight. "I don't even know if Brock loves me, but—I think I might fulfil some need for him, don't you?"

Bunny took the ardent face between her hands and kissed the rounded forehead, a rare gesture for her.

"Yes, my dear, I think you might," she said. "We've never discussed these matters, Sabina, but—I think you know Brock is very dear to me. If you can supply what I've always wanted for him, then—yes, then the end justifies the means."

"Now *you* are talking in riddles," Sabina laughed. "This whole affair is very puzzling and—there's still no reply from Tante."

"Brock will bring news tomorrow," Bunny said.

"Is that where he's been—to the Château Berger?"

"I think quite likely. Oh, dear, now look what I've done! Just as I had them in their right order, too."

The silks had fallen to the floor, where they lay in a tumbled, glowing mass of colour.

"Never mind," Sabina said, stooping to pick them up. "I'll sort them out for you again, and this time we'll put them straight back in their boxes. Isn't it queer, Bunny, that someone as chic and alluring as Madame Jouvez could be fond of a man like M. Bergerac? Perhaps he isn't so elderly and unattractive after all."

"Really, Sabina, you alternate between simple wisdom and utter juvenile nonsense at times!" Bunny sounded quite cross, and Sabina looked surprised.

"Do I?" she said without rancour. "But I still think that was quite a sensible remark. She *is* alluring, even though I didn't like her, and I may have had quite the wrong idea about M. Bergerac."

"Very likely," said Bunny dryly. "Even so, the Bergerac wealth can make up for a great deal to many women, whatever he himself is like. Had you thought of that?"

"Oh!" said Sabina, her eyes widening. "You think it might be Brock she was really fond of, though she wants the Bergerac money more?"

Bunny snatched the skeins of silk from the girl's hands.

"Oh, go to bed, Sabina!" she exclaimed impatiently. "This nonsense leads nowhere, and in any case I've washed my hands of the whole affair. Brock must do his own unravelling—which is more than I can say you have for these silks. They are all snarled up together and I shall need good strong daylight to disentangle them by."

"Poor Bunny, you're tired," Sabina said, and smiled at the look of annoyance on Bunny's face as she remembered how irritating it was to be told this when it was your spirit that was tired rather than your mind.

Was Bunny sad, she wondered, as she undressed that night, at losing her favourite pupil to matrimony at last? Had he all these years filled a place in her heart for the child she had never had, so that now she must suffer the natural pain of relinquishing her rights? Sabina flung open her door as she heard Bunny's step in the passage and stood there, waiting, a candle in her hands.

"Bunny . . ." she said softly, "Bunny darling . . It will make no difference, I promise you You have known a part of him that I can never know. For the rest, we'll share the future—both of us loving him."

The governess paused, shielding her own candle so that the light fell full on her face, revealing its composure; the little rabbit teeth pressed to her lower lip, the round brown eyes mild and a shade reproving. But as she regarded the girl standing there in her long blue robe, the candlelight spilling on her fair and eager face, her expression changed for an instant to one of shy surprise.

"Thank you, my dear; you have a very charming perception. Good night," she said with grave dignity and passed on to her own room.

Sabina returned slowly to hers, and did her nightly round of Brock's mountains, holding the candle above and below the photographs to watch the snowy summits changing in the light. *One day he shall take me*, she thought, *one day when I share a place in his heart with you . . .*

She put out the lamp and before getting into bed she drew the curtains to look out at the night. Moonlight flooded the garden and the old churchyard, bathing the quiet graves in beauty and an unfamiliar sense of peace.

Sabina knew a fleeting regret that it was no longer in her power to bring back order and dignity to Penruthan, but she was not sorry that she would not live there. One woman had stamped sadness upon it while another, in some way bound up with the first, had trespassed with appraising eyes and, like Willie's ghost, left discontent behind. But this was no night for regrets. Even the unpleasant taste left by that strange encounter with Jeanne Jouvez could not spoil the moment, for tomorrow Brock would come, and tomorrow was nearly here . . .

* * *

She wakened to a rough day. It was as if that early spring had been premature and the month of March asserted itself, wiping all traces of tenderness from the earth. A wild wind howled over the moor, bringing sudden squalls of rain, and soot had fallen down the chimney in the night, making black marks on the faded bedroom carpet.

Sabina saw Willie early in the morning, capering on the rough lawn under her window, shouting at the top of his voice:

A knife and a razor
Spells nebuchadnezzar,
A knife and a fork
Spells nebuchadnork;
A new pair of slippers,
And an old pair of shoes——

He broke off abruptly as he saw her leaning out of the window, and with a rude grimace, jumped clumsily over the wall and made off across the moor. It was clearly going to be one of his difficult days.

When she got downstairs the living-room fire was smoking badly, filling the house with acrid fumes, and soot had fallen here, too, covering the furniture with smuts.

"Oh, dear, how tiresome!" Bunny said, exasperated. "The very day that Brock comes back! We shall have to use the parlour, and he says there are no comfortable chairs there."

Smoke filled the house long after the fire had been dowsed and the wind was too strong to permit the opening of windows. Sabina's eyes watered as she helped Bunny with the chores, and Mrs. Cheadle stayed in her kitchen, saying firmly that the smoke would make her cough.

"Why do you keep her?" Sabina asked indignantly, for it had long been apparent that Mrs. Cheadle came only when it suited her, and once there, did little else but drink cups of strong tea over the fire. "There must be other women in the village who'd be glad to work for you and be more help."

"Yes, that's probably true, but Mrs. Cheadle was here in my husband's time. She feels the old rectory is her particular right, and I haven't the heart to make a change," Bunny said, and Sabina smiled at her affectionately. No, she thought, Bunny would not turn Mrs. Cheadle away any more than she would turn away poor simple Willie Washer.

"Where's Willie?" she asked, suddenly missing him. "I saw him early this morning."

"Well, he hasn't come back," Bunny replied. "I'm afraid it's one of those days when everything combines to go wrong, added to which, I've broken my pince-nez."

"Poor Bunny! But never mind, I'll get the wood in for you. Perhaps Willie will come in the afternoon, and then he can clean up the soot on the hearth."

"No, I must do it myself. There's no telling with Willie. Sometimes he stays away for days, and rough weather always seems to affect him."

"Makes him queerer, you mean? I thought he was a little strange yesterday coming back from Penruthan."

They had been upstairs making the beds, and Bunny began to go round the room with her duster while Sabina paused to lean against the window and look out on the wild grey morning.

"Willie thinks Penruthan is haunted," she said. "He talked very strangely on the way home and made a lot of biblical quotations—all foretelling doom, as far as I could make out."

"He has probably got confused with the old stories," Bunny said. "But when he starts quoting from the Bible it usually means he is in for a queer spell."

"What old stories?" asked Sabina. "Do you mean Penruthan *is* supposed to be haunted?"

Bunny straightened a picture and gave a final tweak to the bedspread.

"Not that I've ever heard," she said. "But Willie has grown up with the old traditions, even though he cannot remember the family."

"You mean Madame Bergerac's own family? But that must have been many years ago."

"Yes. But the house remained even if the family was forgotten and—"

"And?" Sabina turned from the window, struck by something strange in Bunny's reply.

Bunny collected her dustpan and brushes and prepared to move into the next room.

"You don't understand country people, my dear," she said. "They accept what they have always known and,

159

especially if they are Cornish, take for granted that others know as much as they do."

Sabina's high forehead creased in perplexity, and the sudden suspicion that she was being warned that she should understand more than she did.

"I don't know what you mean," she said. "Penruthan until now has only been a name to me. Ought I to understand any more than the fact that it was left to me by someone I had never known?"

Bunny stood regarding her, the dustpan in her hands, and her face beneath the knotted handkerchief suddenly tired and uncertain.

"No," she said. "No, Sabina, you are quite right. Penruthan's history concerns you only indirectly and now, perhaps, not at all. Tell me, do you like the house?"

Sabina hesitated. Could one apply such a word to that gaunt, derelict place, beautiful, perhaps, but with a grandeur outmoded and a little sad?

"I don't know," she said slowly. "I would have liked to hand it back to the Bergeracs, but—no, I don't think I would want to live there myself. What will happen to it now?"

Bunny was slow to reply, as if she found the idle question difficult to answer, or distasteful.

"It will, I think, fulfil that for which it was meant," she said at last. "Your hair looks full of soot and smoke. You had better wash it, dear child, before Brock returns."

Sabina did so in the scullery because there the water was hotter, and as she sat drying her hair by the kitchen range while Mrs. Cheadle sniffed and grumbled at the weather, she thought of Bunny's strange remarks, of Willie's oddness and of Jeanne's puzzling behaviour yesterday. Rain beat on the ill-fitting windows which rattled in the wind, and Mrs. Cheadle, rather than exceed her allotted time by five minutes, was already putting on her outdoor clothes to leave, complaining sourly of her wet walk to the village. Sabina did not mind the weather. It was fitting, she thought, that Brock should return on such a day. He was as harsh and forbidding as the elements, and as likely as they to change overnight to a mood of gentleness.

Sabina shook her damp head before the fire, watching drops of water hiss on the red coals. She heard Mrs. Cheadle leave, and settled happily on the rag rug, thankful as Bunny always was to have the kitchen to herself again. A casserole was already in the oven cooking gently for luncheon and the pleasant smell of herbs and onion tickled Sabina's nose and made her hungry.

The back door opened and slammed again, bringing a gust of wind and rain, and Willie Washer stood inside, his heavy boots making muddy marks on the flags.

"What be 'e doin', missy?" he asked.

"Drying my hair. I had to wash it because the living-room smoked ad soot fell down the chimney. If you'd come as usual, Willie, you could have cleaned things up," said Sabina severely. "You were here earlier this morning."

"Can't work outdoors this weather," he said vaguely.

"Then what have you come back for?"

"To see you, mebbe, or that lady."

"What lady?"

"The lady you met to Penruthan, yesterday."

Sabina looked up quickly through the tangle of soft hair.

"Were you spying on us?" she asked quickly. "I thought you said you wouldn't set foot in the house."

He smiled slyly.

"So I never would, but I seed 'e through the windows. Run round, I did, and stood outside the door. I heard 'e talking."

Sabina looked at him uneasily, remembering that he had his queer spells in rough weather.

"Then if you heard us talking you will have understood that we were strangers," she said sharply. "It isn't nice to listen to conversations that aren't meant for your ears, Willie."

"That's how Mis' Fennell talks," he said, unabashed. "That other one with the fiery hair has been there before —I seen 'er."

"She had an order to view," said Sabina. "And I expect you imagined those other times, Willie."

"Nay, I seen 'er. I told 'e the place was 'aunted."

"Oh, I see. Well, she wasn't a ghost. She's a—friend of Mr. Brock's. I don't suppose she'll come back. She didn't like Penruthan much."

"She'll come back—like the other foreign lady who died."

Sabina shook back her hair and smiled at him. She could see what Bunny had meant when she said that Willie had probably got confused with the old stories.

"That was Madame Bergerac," she said gently. "And she wasn't really a foreigner, you know. Did you think it was she who haunted Penruthan?"

He looked vague, then nodded his head slowly.

"Well, that's foolish, Willie," Sabina said. "The first lady died and left the house to me, so she wouldn't want to come back, would she? And the foreign lady you saw yesterday won't come again, for the house isn't for sale."

"It don't belong to you," Willie said with sudden anger. " 'Tes Maister Brock should have it."

"Mr. Brock!" Sabina looked startled, then she remembered the boy's fondness for Brock, who was always gentle with him. "Mr. Brock couldn't afford to live there any more than I could. Don't worry, Willie; no strangers shall have it. It will just stay empty—with the ghosts, if it has any."

" 'Tes cursed," he said with stubborn solemnity. "If Maister Brock can't have 'e, no one shall."

"No one will," she said gently. "Take your boots off, Willie, and sit by the fire. Mrs. Fennell will let you have some stew later. Doesn't it smell good?"

" 'Tes cursed," he said again, and, turning, shuffled out of the kitchen with never another word.

Sabina reported the conversation to Bunny as they ate their luncheon, but Bunny, instead of smiling, looked slightly worried.

"Willie has not had one of these spells for a long time," she said. "I wonder if I ought to go down to the village and have a word with that old aunt he lives with."

"Oh, Bunny, not on a day like this!" protested Sabina. "You'll get blown off your feet. Willie often talks a little strangely—it's nothing to worry about, surely?"

"Perhaps not, but all the same—it was a pity you persuaded him to take you to Penruthan, Sabina. It's probably started the old train of thought again."

"That it really should belong to Brock? But that's very natural, Bunny. He's fond of Brock, and you said yourself he had probably got confused with the old history. I believe he thinks Madame Jouvez and Madame Bergerac are the same person, though he can't ever have known Madame Bergerac, can he?"

"No. He was a baby when she died, still—"

Sabina experienced a moment of disquiet; it was unlike Bunny to fuss. Still, the mishaps of the morning had probably upset her and she was on edge.

"Wait till Brock comes back. If you still think it's necessary to go to the village, he can take you in the car," Sabina said, and a small spring of excitement bubbled up inside her as she glanced at the clock. In another hour he would be here and she would know again the assuring touch of his hands and the hard pressure of his lips.

Bunny saw the ardent happiness in the girl's young face and smiled.

"It stopped raining. Go down to the gates and watch for him when the time comes," she said.

*   *   *

But he took her unaware just the same. His train must have been early or she late in starting, and she did not hear the sound of the taxi in the high wind that was blowing. She had taken the short cut through the churchyard, lingering to read the epitaphs on the graves, and he came up behind her, making her start violently as he took her without warning by the shoulders.

For a moment her old distaste for the graveyard returned in superstitious force, and as she looked up into the dark, forbidding face with the saturnine lift to the eyebrows, there was a hint of panic in her eyes.

"Well!" he said with the remembered irony. "They say that Satan's always behind you. You're looking at me as if you think I'm the old gentleman himself!"

"You frightened me," she said, "and—you do look rather like Satan among all these creepy tombstones."

"The devil, I imagine, would fight shy of churchyards,"

163

he replied dryly. "Is that the only greeting you have for me, Miss Lamb?"

She had forgotten how much at a disadvantage he could make her feel. During the past week she had remembered only that he had wanted her, that whatever the limitations of his own more experienced feelings might be, for her he had filled a niche which had been empty since childhood.

"Are you well?" she asked shyly. "Did you have a pleasant journey?"

"How very correct and polite! Bunny would approve," he said, then put a hand under her chin, tilting up her face and his eyes were suddenly tender.

"I believe you're shy," he said softly as he kissed her.

The wind swooped between the graves, flattening her against him and she suddenly flung her arms about his neck, yielding with a passion that had desire only for the moment.

"That's better," he said. "I was beginning to think you had thought better of your decision of a week ago and were hankering for the unknown charms of M. Bergerac."

"Am I wise to forget him?" she laughed, half angry that he was still at his old trick of dragging René Bergerac into the most promising occasions.

"Perhaps not," he replied, a hint of laughter in his voice. "How good your hair smells. What have you been doing to it?"

"Only washing it. It was full of soot and smoke because this wind has brought disaster to the living-room chimney, and Bunny has broken her pince-nez and is very upset."

"Poor Bunny. We had better go in and soothe her."

They walked back to the house, and Sabina saw that Brock was using a stick for the first time.

"Is your leg worse?" she asked quickly.

"Oh, no," he replied. "But a little support speeds up progress. I can't depend on that willing but not very adequate shoulder of yours all the time, can I?"

She knew he was thinking of that slow, painful walk home in the snow and said, because sooner or later such things must be said between them:

"Bunny once told me you were afraid of pity. To help

someone you—you love is not pity, and the helper shouldn't be insulted by such compassion. My shoulder will always be there, Brock."

He did not answer sharply, as he would have done before, but said with grave attention:

"I know, Sabina. The fact that I can accept your compassion with humility should tell you a great deal."

The wind had whipped colour into her thin cheeks and she looked up at him with inquiring and suddenly brilliant eyes, but he only smiled and, opening the rectory door, stood aside to let her pass in.

Bunny gave Brock her usual warm but restrained greeting, but she still seemed put out by the small household mishaps and apologised repeatedly for the enforced use of the parlour, which had no comfortable chairs.

"This is unlike you, Bunny," Brock said at last. "You and I have picnicked in more uncomfortable situations than this. If it's only the chairs that worry you, we can shift something in from the other room."

"I'm being foolish," she apologised. "I think this high wind must have made me nervous, and I'm a little anxious about Willie."

"Willie Washer? What's he been up to?"

"Nothing, I hope, but I think he's working up for one of his spells. Sabina persuaded him to take her across the moor to Penruthan yesterday, and I'm afraid it upset him."

Brock's cool blue eyes went to Sabina's face.

"A final check-up before throwing away your inheritance?" he inquired, and she flushed.

"No," she replied. "And I'm not throwing away an inheritance. Since I'm not marrying M. Bergerac it's mine whether I like it or not."

"True," he observed. "And what will you do with it?"

"Willie thinks I should give it to you," she said, and Bunny made a small gesture of impatience.

"This whole affair has gone far enough, Brock," she said. "Now you've presumably settled your—your business, we should all know where we stand."

"Is that what's making you jumpy?" he asked. "All in good time, my dear; I've only just walked into the house."

He began to fill a pipe, and as the front-door bell rang Bunny exclaimed crossly:

"Now who can that be in the middle of the afternoon?"

"I'll go," said Sabina. "It might be news of Willie."

There was, indeed, no reason why there should be news of Willie, who had been talking to her in the kitchen only at lunchtime, but Sabina thought it best to try to get rid of the unwanted caller if she could. It was no time to be forced into a discussion on mundane affairs with Mrs. Weymouth or one of the ladies of the parish.

But the visitor was not of the parish. She had tied a chiffon scarf over her flaming hair to protect it from the wind, but even with her back to the door that tall, elegant figure was unmistakable.

"What can I do for you, Madame Jouvez?" Sabina asked quietly.

"I have come to see Blaireau. I am expected, yes?" Jeanne Jouvez said.

"I don't think so, but Brock has only just arrived."

"No matter. We are old friends, and Madame *la gouvernante* would not refuse me a moment's hospitality. This is her house, I think?"

Although the last sentence was phrased as a question, Sabina knew that it was she who was being put in her place.

"Of course," she said. "Will you come in?"

she had no chance to warn Bunny, for Jeanne was close on her heels. She could catch the scent of her heavy French perfume as she opened the parlour door.

"Madame Jouvez seemed to think she was expected," Sabina said, and saw the almost comic outrage in Bunny's mild eyes as she bowed stiffly to the newcomer.

"Madame . . ." murmured Jeanne in acknowledgment, "and Blaireau . . . It is an inconvenient moment, yes? You would prefer that I call another time?"

Brock stood, his pipe in his hand, and looked at her steadily without moving. If he was pleased, annoyed, or merely surprised, he gave no sign. Only his eyebrows lifted a little higher at the corners and his eyes were frosty and intensely blue.

"I didn't know you were still in England, Jeanne," he said. "Let me introduce Mrs. Fennell and Miss Sabina Lamb."

166

"Mademoiselle and I have already met—at Penruthan," Jeanne said, seating herself unasked in a chair by the fire.

"Penruthan!"

"She did not tell you?"

"There's scarcely been time," said Sabina quickly, noticing Brock's frown.

"And you talked of—?" he inquired with a dispassionate courtesy which carried a warning note of steel.

"Of many things, *chérie*," Jeanne replied looking up through her lashes. "Mademoiselle is, I think, a little confused in her notions."

"I thought I had at least made matters clear to *you* when we met," Brock said, and Sabina, knowing now that the woman had simply come to make mischief, broke gently into the little exchange.

"You don't need to enlighten my ignorance, madame," she said. "It was quite clear that there had been a—a fondness between you and Brock in the past, but that has nothing to do with me."

"This is embarrassing!" Bunny exclaimed. It was long past tea-time and growing dark, but she had no intention of extending her hospitality further. "Sabina, I think it would be better if you and I let these two settle their— differences in private. Come, my dear."

"No, no, no," said Jeanne, but the amusement in her eyes held a glint of spite. "I would not put you to an inconvenience, madame; besides, there are matters we should all discuss."

"I think not," said Brock with icy politeness. "These matters, as you call them, no longer concern you, and I prefer to do things in my own way."

"Very possibly," she retorted, undisturbed. "But you, my friend, cannot play one woman off against another and keep them both."

"You and I settled that question long ago," he said wearily. "I have never tried to keep you, Jeanne; marriage didn't enter into our scheme of things."

"Perhaps not in yours," she snapped with sudden malice. Sabina said gently:

"It was René Bergerac you hoped to marry, so I understood yesterday. I thought I had made it clear that I was no longer in the way."

Bunny's distress was now plain for all to see, and she made a small, futile gesture towards Jeanne.

"Madame . . ." she said, but Jeanne took no notice of her. Her long, brilliant eyes travelled over Sabina's slender immature body, then she flung back her head and laughed.

"Oh, my poor innocent!" she said. "So much in love with the good Blaireau, and what will you say when you find how you have been deceived? What will you do when you find that, after all, a heartless man can win in a few short weeks the final seal to a bargain?"

"I don't understand you," said Sabina, moving instinctively nearer to Bunny who put out a distressed hand.

"No? Well, you have been used very cleverly, *ma petite*, and I, for one, will have much interest in finding out how far you can be tricked in this affair."

Brock had not spoken, and she turned to him suddenly, with an amused air of exasperation.

"How much longer is this farce to continue, René? Until Lucille Lamb returns with the marriage settlement and there is no turning back?"

There was an instant's pregnant silence while the wind rattled at the windows and the shabby, old-fashioned furniture and the faded papered walls of the parlour had a moment of unreality.

"René?" said Sabina, her voice sounding curiously loud.

"Yes, my child," said Jeanne with a careless snap of the fingers. "It is as well to know which of them you are marrying, for René Bergerac and our good Blaireau are one and the same person."

CHAPTER TEN

NOBODY spoke, then Brock knocked out his pipe with a sharp sound of finality and Sabina looked at him.

"Is that true?" she asked.

He put his hands in his pockets and surveyed her reflectively. He was neither disconcerted nor in any hurry to offer explanations.

"Yes," he replied. "Should it make any difference?"

"But I don't understand," Sabina said. "Why did you call yourself by a different name?"

"The name happens to be mine," he said. "I'm old René Bergerac's stepson, of which fact your otherwise careful aunt was apparently unaware. Would you prefer it if I were French?"

His tone was light and ironical, as if the whole question was of no importance, and Sabina's young mouth looked suddenly hurt.

"Did you do it for amusement—to see how far you could upset Tante's plans before telling me the truth?" she asked.

"He did it because he knows well his attraction for women and wished to be quite sure of Penruthan," observed Jeanne, enjoying the situation she had created. "It was not difficult to fall in love with him, was it, mademoiselle? You know nothing of men, my poor child, or the lengths they will go to for something they want. As you suggested yourself, it will have had its amusing side, too."

Bunny spoke for the first time, and her voice was a little unsteady.

"You have done enough damage by your interference, madame. I would be glad if you would go now," she said.

"But perhaps I am not ready to leave," Jeanne retorted with lazy insolence, and Bunny replied:

"This happens to be my house, and I do not care to have you any longer under my roof."

Even Jeanne recognised the old schoolroom authority and rose to her feet without hurry.

"As you please," she said with a shrug. "Au 'voir, mademoiselle. Perhaps I have saved you from making a fool of yourself, *hein*?"

"You can say the rest to me—outside," said Brock quite pleasantly, and placing a hand under her elbow thrust her firmly from the room.

Sabina's face still had that frozen look of helplessness which Jeanne's remarks had put there. Seeing it, Bunny said:

"Don't take it badly, my dear. She's gone now. When Brock comes back he will explain things to you."

"There's nothing left to explain, now, is there?" Sabina answered with careful politeness, then the stillness went from her face and gave place to pain and a bitter humilation.

"*You* knew, Bunny," she accused. "You could have saved me from making a fool of myself, instead of Madame Jouvez, only you didn't choose. Like Brock, I suppose you wanted to be sure of Penruthan."

Bunny's eyes were suddenly reproving, and she automatically felt for the pince-nez which were normally pinned to her dress.

"That does not seem logical, dear child," she observed. "When you came here you were resigned to marrying a man you had never met, knowing the position about Penruthan. The fact that he and Brock are the same person should make things easier, surely? You had not, after all, reckoned on falling in love with René Bergerac."

"But can't you see—can't you *see* what he's done to me?"

"I cannot see, except for the untimely interference of a malicious woman, that it can make the smallest difference. Brock would have told you himself today."

Sabina was crying, rubbing the tears from her cheeks and lashes with helpless, impotent gestures.

"It was different before," she said. "But to make me love him, and laugh at me all the time, was—was—"

Bunny touched her gently.

"Oh, my dear, that's not true. I confess at the beginning I had doubts because—well, I'm afraid your aunt had read more into the situation than was warranted. We kept you here because—well, because we thought you de-

170

served a chance of finding your own feet, and then—he fell in love with you."

"No. He realised that, as Madame Jouvez said, a heartless man can accomplish more in a few short weeks—when he has someone young and inexperienced to deal with," said Sabina bitterly.

Bunny sighed. The young were so headstrong, so ignorant of shades and subtleties.

"Listen, Sabina—let me tell you something of Brock's early life," she said, and stopped automatically to make up the fire. The familiar homely gesture brought fresh tears to Sabina's eyes and she knelt on the hearth to help.

"Brock was only three when his mother married M. Bergerac and took him to France. The old man delighted in the child, insisted on giving him his name and, no doubt, spoilt him. Later, when the marriage had not turned out well, Madame Bergerac returned to England to live at Penruthan. I was governess there, and I think the boy, too young to understand his mother's situation, fretted for the Château Berger and his gay, wealthy stepfather. The Brockmans were poor, and Brock and his mother lived in one wing of the house, and she, poor lady, became a recluse with less and less time to give to a growing child. When Brock was older he insisted on spending a portion of the year with his stepfather, who looked on him as his own son, hoping he would follow him in the business. He took pride in being known in France as young René Bergerac and when, later, he came into the business it was quite natural and better for trade to be known by his stepfather's famous name. There are probably few people in France who remember that Brock is not old René's son, and when he is over here—well, he finds it restful to be himself and revert to his proper name. You see, he realised too late that all his boyhood he had sided against his mother, and her action in leaving Penruthan away from the family was not spite, as many people think, but a final renunciation of everything she had thought belonged to her and her child. Not very logical, you think, perhaps, but she was very melancholy towards the end, poor thing, and there was no one to advise her."

Sabina listened, still kneeling on the hearth, an apple-bough in her hands. So much was explained: the pair of *armoires*, one at Penruthan, one at the rectory, Brock's strange familiarity with the house, his oblique defence of the mother he had misjudged, his contempt for Lucille Faivre, who had contributed so much towards misunderstanding in two generations. Above all, was not the explanation of Tante's behaviour plain? Tante entering into the conspiracies, taking orders from the man who had so strangely crossed their paths . . . But she could not see, in the raw state of her shocked mind, that, for Brock, what had started as a diversion and an irresistible urge to upset the apple cart might have ended, as it had for her, in a more serious engagement of the emotions. He had never said he loved her; he had not, even now, sought in any way to soften the shock of Jeanne's disclosures.

Sabina placed the wood carefully on the fire and immediately the nostalgic scent of burning apple filled the room, reminding her of those snowy evenings when she and Brock had sat alone by the fire and her love had blossomed shyly and begun to grow.

"Were there, then, no negotiations? Did Tante invent it all?" she asked wearily.

"Not all," replied Bunny gently. "Your aunt had made tentative proposals, and Brock, familiar with the old tradition, was willing to meet her, but he is not French, and certainly not the man to take a wife in order to acquire a house."

"Then why couldn't he have said so when that Jouvez woman was making things so hideously plain?" Sabina said, springing suddenly to her feet. "He stood there as if nothing mattered—as if all she said was true!"

"My dear Sabina!" Bunny reproved. "Brock would scarcely indulge in—er—tender scenes in front of a woman of that kind."

"Why wouldn't he?" demanded Sabina. "Because he was once fond of her? Because he doesn't really care what happens to me? He's never told me once he loved me. He doesn't—he only loves the mountains and—and himself!"

She ran out of the room before Bunny could reply, desiring now only to get out of the house and into the

172

wild March weather before Brock returned. But she was not quick enough. She met him in the living-room, and he took her by the wrist as she tried to slip past him.

"Running away again?" he said.

His black hair was ruffled by the wind and his hands felt cold and harsh. Whatever the outcome of his private intercourse with Jeanne, his dark face was forbidding, with no hint of tenderness for Sabina as he forced her to meet his eyes.

"Running away? Yes, why not?" she said, accepting the suggestion with defiant relief.

"Because a clever woman can make trouble for you so easily? I thought you were more sane than that, Sabina."

"You thought I was a fool, as she said. You thought it would be amusing to shake my faith in Tante's arrangements and get what you wanted at the same time."

"Is that what you really think?"

"What else should I think?" she cried. "You and Bunny playing a game of your own, and I young enough and silly enough to fall for it!"

The familiar room seemed forbidding and unfriendly with the cold ruin of the morning's fire and a thin trickle of light coming from the hall. The smell of soot still hung in the air and the wind roaring down the vast chimney brought fresh falls to settle on the hearth. She felt Brock's fingers tighten on her wrists, drawing her closer, and she was unable to resist, though her body instantly stiffened.

"Yes, you are young and silly, my foolish lamb," he said, his voice suddenly gentle. "Why should the truth make any difference? You didn't love poor M. Bergerac—you hadn't even met him, though you were willing to marry him."

But M. Bergerac was no longer a joke he could fall back upon when it suited him.

"That's Bunny's argument," she said with hardness. "Neither of you seem to understand that falling in love alters everything."

"Does it?"

"Yes, it does. At least you never pretended you loved me—at any rate not really, but now—well, everything's different. I suppose there's nothing to stop me making over Penruthan to you, is there?"

His eyes were frosty and unrevealing in his dark face.

"Do you not intend, then, to honour your part of the bargain?" he asked coolly.

"No," she said, and the bitter humiliation of her hurt swamped the earlier felicity of the day. "You and Tante laughing together over my silly letters which cost such a lot to write—when all the time you knew it was a game . . . No wonder Tante was so obliging . . . no wonder poor faithful Marthe couldn't understand . . . Willie Washer wasn't so simple when he thought Penruthan should belong to you, was he? These country people have known and accepted you all along, I suppose. Only I was the credulous fool . . ."

He was silent, watching her tears, then he put out a gentle hand to brush them away.

"I've hurt you very much, haven't I?" he said.

She made no answer and suddenly, abruptly, he let her go.

"Finish your weeping alone," he said wearily. "This, it would seem, is no time to reason with you."

He watched her run from the room and listened to the sound of her light feet on the stairs, then he went back to the parlour and Bunny.

The governess sat by the fire on one of the hard, upright chairs, her hands folded impotently in her lap. She had lighted the lamp, and in its radiance her face looked tired and pinched. She had heard Sabina's raised voice in the next room and the abrupt slamming of the door.

"Well, Brock," she said, "I'm afraid you took too many chances. You should at least have made sure that Madame Jouvez had returned to France."

"Is that your oblique way of saying 'I told you so'?" he asked.

"No, but I never did approve of this deception. Have you made no effort to explain your own feelings to the child?"

He sat down wearily, stretching his lame leg stiffly before him.

"It was hardly the time or the place in that chilly room of yours with soot blowing down the chimney," he retorted. "In any case she was not in a receptive mood."

174

"That's scarcely to be wondered at," Bunny commented dryly. "You made little effort to take the sting out of that unpleasant young woman's observations."

"What do you take me for?" he inquired harshly. "The damage was done. It wasn't going to help anyone to explain or expostulate then."

"So I tried to tell Sabina, but she's at the age when a fine show of feeling counts a great deal."

He raised his eyebrows.

"I gave her credit for more sense," he said shortly, and Bunny patted her neatly netted hair with a small, ineffectual movement.

"My dear boy! I think you've expected more maturity from poor Sabina than it's as yet in her power to give," she said. "She told me you have never once said that you—er—loved her—in fact you loved only the mountains and yourself."

He rubbed his eyelids with a tired, nervous gesture.

"Oh, heavens, Bunny, what did she expect!" he exclaimed irritably. "Doesn't a woman know what a man feels for her without being told?"

Her smile was the one she used to bestow on him when as a small boy he had been particularly stubborn.

"I don't know," she said with a certain primness; "but I can imagine women like to hear it in so many words. That's only natural."

He grinned at her suddenly

"I had thought there was plenty of time for that. We hadn't even reached the formality of being engaged," he said.

"But you do love her, Brock?"

She asked the question with delicate diffidence because she had always considered such probings to be an impertinence, but his eyes held a tender affection as he replied gently:

"Yes, dear Bunny; I've learnt the wisdom of your counsels."

"That there are other ways of fulfilment besides climbing mountains."

"Then see that she knows it too, dear boy. The young are very vulnerable, and I believe first love must be handled with care. Where is she?"

175

"Crying in her room, I imagine, and probably packing a suitcase."

Bunny looked alarmed.

"You mean you think she might run away?"

"Well, she has a weakness for it, hasn't she? Especially running away from the man she's suppoed to marry! Don't worry, Bunny. It's a rough evening, and she won't get far, carrying a heavy suitcase. We'll hear her go if she does. Incidentally, you don't need to worry about Willie's whereabouts. He was lurking among the graves when I had my little plain speaking with Jeanne. I shouted to him when she had gone, but he went over the wall to the moor looking as if he'd seen a ghost."

"He saw her at Penruthan yesterday," Bunny said absently. "I think he confuses her with your mother, who he is convinced haunts the place."

"Perhaps she does," he said, sounding suddenly tired. "Perhaps Penruthan is best left to rot in its decay."

"Was that the front door?" Bunny got to her feet, but he smiled at her reassuringly.

"No, my silly dear, it was the wind. Don't fuss—I shall hear her if she goes."

* * *

But they neither of them heard her. Bunny dropped into a fitful doze and Brock, brooding on his own follies, became used to the noises of the house and ceased to separate one sound from another. Sabina crept out of the house an hour later and began the long walk to the little railway halt beyond the village.

Her bout of weeping over, it had not taken her long to decide what she must do. To stay another night at the rectory was impossible after what had occurred. Had Brock taken her in his arms and replied to Jeanne Jouvez' taunts, or later sought to comfort instead of telling her to finish her weeping alone, she could have tried to listen with reason to the explanations Bunny had started in the parlour, but he had made it only too plain that he found her attitude illogical, that she had no more right to expect tenderness from him than from the mythical René Bergerac.

176

She could not pack everything into one suitcase, but they would, perhaps, send the rest after her. When she reached Marthe at the address of her Hampstead friends she would write, tendering gratitude for her visit and apologies for causing so much trouble. She did not want to go to Marthe, but there was no one else. Very shortly now, Tante must return following the successful culmination of her plans, and Tante, too, must be faced and the endless, weary scenes and arguments.

Sabina looked anxiously in her purse, counting the money which Bunny had said Tante had sent for her. There was just enough for a single third-class fare to London, but poor Willie would have to go without his present. She thought of Willie as she packed, while Brock's cold mountains looked down at her from the walls. It seemed so long ago now that the tow-headed boy had stood in the kitchen in his muddy boots and told her that Penruthan was cursed. Well, perhaps it was. It had brought the Bergeracs no happiness and certainly none to her, for those brief days of felicity had been bound not with the house, but with Brock whom she had thought to be poor and without guile.

She shut the bulging case, fastening the locks with difficulty. He should have his house. If it was legally possible to give Penruthan away she would return it to the only person who had a right to it, but she would not barter herself now to a man who did not love her. When she was ready to leave she stood for a moment, bidding a silent farewell to the room. She gazed longest at Kanchenjunga with its five snow summits. It had always been her favourite of them all, and she lifted a mocking hand in salute.

"You win," she said softly and turned to go.

The wind took her as she went down the drive, whipping her clothes like paper to her body, and buffeting the suitcase against her legs. It was very dark and the tombstones in the graveyard sprang like gaunt spectres from the shadows. The wind sighed through the long grass between the graves, and beyond, the moor was a vast pool of blackness.

Sabina battled with difficulty against the wind, stopping every so often to change the heavy suitcase from one hand

177

to the other. As she went down the deserted road to the village, Willie's tune came unbidden to her mind, and accompanied her flagging footsteps in the darkness:

> *Willie Washer's proper mazed,*
> *Doesn't know where he was raised . . .*

A stone had got into her shoe, and she had to prop herself on the high, crumbling bank in order to remove it:

> *Silly Willie proper dazed,*
> *Sillie Willie Wash-er*

Poor Willie, she thought, her arm aching painfully, he would be disappointed that she had forgotten his present and left without bidding him good-bye.

The village seemed deserted, too. Only the little inn showed a bright light of invitation over its door, but no one went in or out. Sabina felt exhausted. The day's emotions had drained her, and the wind and her encumbering suitcase had taken the last of her strength. The little halt was still a long way off at the top of the steep hill beyond the village; she could not, she thought, carry the suitcase any further. She left it on the little green outside the inn and walked on. Someone would find it and take it back to the rectory.

When at last she reached the halt she was fighting for breath and her legs felt as if they no longer belonged to her. The old porter who was sole guardian of Truan station knew her by sight and seemed amazed by her demand for a single ticket to London.

"Lunnon!" he said, "you'll not get there tonight. Connection for the six o'clock from Kairy went at four. Did 'e walk up here, missy?"

"Yes. Isn't there a train at all?"

"There's the midnight, but connection from here don't go till ten."

"What's the time now?"

He peered at an ancient turnip watch the size of a saucer.

"Seven fifty-eight pre-cisely," he announced in tones which sounded as if he expected her to contradict him immediately. "What be the rectory folk a-thinkin' of to let 'e walk on a night like this?" He thrust a whiskered face suddenly into hers and added suspiciously: "Do they know you'm goin' to Lunnon?"

"Yes . . . yes . . ." said Sabina hurriedly. "Can I have my ticket please?"

He produced one reluctantly and took her money, then came out of his small wooden cabin to lock the gates.

"Can't wait here," he said. "No train for two hours, and I be goin' home for me bite."

Sabina looked at the dark countryside, which offered no shelter, and despair made her want to cry all over again.

"But can't I wait on the platform?" she pleaded. "I must—I *must* sit down. I can't walk about for two hours."

"Well—" he scratched his head, giving her a very old-fashioned look at the same time. "I don't never allow it when I'm not about, but—well, p'raps you'd best sit in the shelter, but no larking on the line, mind you, like they dratted boys. If I find you been up to tricks I'll be powerful angry."

Sabina laughed a little hysterically.

"I don't feel at all like larking on the line," she said, and he let her through to the platform and locked her in.

There was a rough wooden shelter with one bench, and she sank on to it thankfully. As she stretched her aching legs, rubbing the calves, in which pins and needles had started little points of pain, she thought of Brock spending his boyhood in Penruthan, living in one wing with only his mother and governess for company. Had he felt bitter when she, an interloper, had come to inspect the house he knew so well, or had he listened to her comments with tolerance, knowing that through her he could get his home back again? Had he been happy with no companions with whom to share the walled-in gardens, or had he been impatient for the moment when his exile was over and he could return to his stepfather's comfortable château in France? It no longer mattered, she supposed, and whatever ties there were with the past, all that remained now to Penruthan was its use commercially.

As time went on and only the wind howled through the darkness, Sabina came to know a great desolation. It seemed to her that she must be the only creature left alive in this isolation of blackness; no trains had ever passed this way, no train ever would; she was condemned to sit here for ever and no one would come to unlock the gates.

She must have fallen asleep, for she did not hear Brock's dragging steps on the wooden platform, nor was she aware of him standing there looking down at her until the beam from his torch flashed in her face. For a moment she thought it was that other occasion when he had found her asleep in the snow at Penruthan, and she murmured, as then:

"I came straight across the moor, going west . . ."

He bent over her and roughly shook her awake.

"You have a genius for causing alarm and despondency in people's otherwise quiet homes, haven't you?" he said, and she blinked up at him, shocked back into the reality of the moment.

"I might have known that you would catch up with me before I had a chance," she sighed.

"A chance for what? To arrive in London in the small hours with no luggage and nowhere to go?"

"I was going to Marthe. I would have written."

"How thoughtful of you. And did you suppose that the estimable Marthe wouldn't have sent you straight back here?"

"No, why should she? She didn't like you. She thought you would interfere with Tante's plans."

"Very likely," he retorted with extreme dryness. "But it must be presumed that by now your aunt has communicated with her devoted servant and made everything clear."

"Oh!" said Sabina. "I hadn't thought of that."

She glanced at him a little timidly. He seemed as she remembered him first at Kairy with a hat pulled over his eyes and the collar of an old raincoat turned up to meet it. It would not have surprised her if he had suddenly offered her a glass of brandy.

"What do you want me to do?" she asked with the reasonableness of utter defeat.

"I seem to remember telling you when I left that the next time you ran away you would have to be punished. What would you suggest—an old-fashioned spanking, or just exiled to France with an unsympathetic husband?"

She did not reply, but only gave him a faint, uncertain smile, and he sat down beside her on the hard, shiny bench and studied his hands clasped between his knees.

"Sabina—" he said, and the harshness had gone from his voice, "I've been foolish with you, I think. I let this business go too far, as Bunny pointed out. Tell me—if you had learnt the truth from me today, as I had intended, and not from Jeanne, would you have had this violent reaction?"

His closeness made it difficult to reply with honesty.

"Perhaps not," she said. "You would have—kept the illusion for me, I think; but she—she took everything away."

"And yet you were willing to marry René Bergerac to start with—knowing just those same things."

"Yes," she said, "I suppose it *is* illogical, as Bunny said; but you see, I had never been in love. I didn't know that—that things would hurt when before—well, I suppose I was just callow and—it's very hard for me to explain, Brock."

He looked at her then. She wore a little knitted cap of blue wool pulled down over her ears. Beneath it the pale, soft hair turned outwards in charming disorder like a very young child's.

"You don't have to explain," he said gently. "It's I who should do that, for I always understood. I knew from the first that you weren't the sort to be married off in that high-handed fashion with any success. Do you really think it was the house I was after?"

Her rounded forehead creased in perplexity. She was very tired.

"I don't know," she said. "It's difficult to divide you. René Bergerac is nothing like I imagined, and he at any rate wanted Penruthan."

"But he was an elderly *roué*, fat and shiny with a weak digestion—remember?"

She smiled.

"I suppose it was fun," she said a little bitterly, "describing yourself in unattractive terms and—and reminding me of M. Bergerac at most awkward moments."

"Of course it was fun. Must it all come to an end?"

"What do you mean?"

"Well, in England, M. Bergerac can still be a very good joke, and in France—well, we might have some laughs

181

at the expense of that overbearing Mr. Brockman, mightn't we?"

"Oh, Brock!" She leant her head against his shoulder and knew that she was beaten.

"You don't have to marry me, you know," he said, his voice suddenly harsh. "Whatever the necessity for an English branch of Berger, there is no need to go to that extreme."

"I was going to make the house over to you anyway, if it was legally possible," she said. "If you will take me as well—then, I suppose, as Bunny says, logically things shouldn't be any different. Willie said you should have it, anyway."

"And why should you make such momentous decisions on the strength of the wandering of poor simple Willie Washer?" He spoke flippantly because for him the moment held a sudden poignancy.

"I don't know," she replied quite seriously, "but he's been in my mind all day, and I can't get that horrid rhyme the children used to sing at him out of my head."

The old porter appeared at the entrance of the shelter, a hurricane lamp in his hand.

"Be 'e goin' to stay here all night, zur?" he said disapprovingly. "You told me you was only fetching the little maid home and you'm been here a quarter hour."

"I'm sorry, Smale; we're going now," Brock said and got up, extending a hand to Sabina.

"Won't be no one for ten o'clock now. Might as well go 'ome," the porter said. "Powerful big fire somewheres, zur. I doubt me if they'll get 'er under in this wind."

He pointed to the sky, which showed a dull glow on the horizon of the moor. Every so often tongues of brightness lit the darkness and died again.

"Where is it, do you know?" Brock asked, but the old man shook his head.

"Hard to say. Could be over to Pennytor or the old timber yard beyond the cross-roads. By the time fire brigade gets out from Kairy 'twill all be over, I reckon. Now, missy, here's your fare back, and I'll trouble you for that ticket. Don't get playing they tricks again. Goin' to Lunnon by the midnight and coming two hours early for the train!"

He let them out by the little wicket gate, locked it after them and stumped off into the darkness.

"What happens if someone gets off the ten o'clock?" asked Sabina.

"No one will. Smale knows the habits and destinations of every passenger on this line."

"He told me," Sabina giggled, "not to have larks on the line. As if I felt like it!"

"No, your larks take other forms," he replied a trifle grimly as they found the car. "Get in."

"That photograph," she said inconsequently, "it was—was—misleading, wasn't it?"

"Very glamorous," he replied with a smile, "but I prefer the original."

"Do you?" asked Sabina dubiously. "Do you really?"

"Yes, my modest lamb, I do. I can find pictures like that in any of the glossy magazines," he said.

"And the cooking you were so good at—should I have known who you were, then?"

"Not necessarily. In fact you thought I had a job in some scrubby little restaurant, didn't you? Well, perhaps I have. A good *hotelier* must know what goes on in his own kitchens. I have my stepfather to thank for that. Anything else you want to know?"

"No. None of it matters, really," she said disconsolately, and he started his engine, his profile in the darkness blurred and unapproachable.

When they reached the village, Sabina remembered her suitcase.

"It's been found," Brock told her with a certain asperity. "And really, Sabina, you have a most haphazard way of going about things. When you arrive you leave your luggage in the train, and when you leave, you dump it outside a pub."

"I couldn't carry it any further," she said. "I suppose that put you on my trail."

"Not a very difficult trail to follow with your marked propensity for running away," he replied, then gave her a quick sidelong glance. "It did occur to me, you know, that you might have picked up another stranger at the pub and accepted a lift in your trusting fashion."

He spoke with his usual irony, but for the first time she realised that he had been anxious about her, that under his whole manner had lain a tension she had been too tired to see.

"I'm sorry," she said and wanted to say more, but he stopped the car outside the inn, where a knot of villagers had gathered to watch the glow of the fire in the sky, much nearer now and infinitely brighter.

"Where is it, do you know?" Brock called out of the window and a man detached himself from the others to come and speak to him.

"They do say 'tes Penruthan, zur," he said.

"Penruthan! But it's empty."

"Well, 'tes the right direction and there's no other big place that way. Best get up there, Mr. Brockman, zur, and see, though there'll not be much you can do."

Brock slammed in the gears and the car leapt forward down the road.

*　　　*　　　*

He drove past the rectory turning and up the hill to the road across the moor.

"If it really is Penruthan, someone's been causing mischief," he observed grimly. "There are no fires or electricity there."

Was this to be the final blow? Sabina wondered wearily. Was she to lose, after all, the inheritance that was to buy her way to his affections?

"But who would do a thing like that?" she asked reasonably, and suddenly knew he was thinking of Jeanne Jouvez. She began to laugh, and he said sharply:

"You have an odd sense of humour. Arson isn't very pretty, and it may happen to be your own property that's in danger."

"It wasn't that," she said. "But I couldn't imagine Madame Jouvez gliding gracefully through the house in her elegant clothes, pouring petrol over everything, however much she was tempted to remove the obstructions to what she wants."

He smiled faintly in the darkness.

"So you knew what I was thinking?" he said. "Yes, of course you're right. Jeanne is hardly cast for such dra-

184

He looked at her with eyes that were hard and brilliant. They were both beginning to cough with the smoke.

"All right, call the men, and then get to hell out of here," he said tensely.

"There's no time," she replied. "Besides, he knows me."

"Not you, Sabina," he said roughly. "It's getting too dangerous. I'll go alone."

"No," she said stubbornly. "You might forget the tune!"

He took her hand, holding it firmly, and his eyes were suddenly the far-seeing, dispassionate eyes of the mountaineer who recognises and accepts danger for himself and those in his charge.

"Very well. How does it go?" he said.

"Willie Washer's proper mazed . . ." Hand in hand they began pacing the empty rooms, their voices echoing eerily. Outside the sound of the wind and the flames mingled indistinguishably, and smoke was starting to seep through the cracks in the walls ". . . silly Willie, proper dazed . . ." they were in a long corridor now, filled with discarded packing-cases; there was the sound of a furtive movement at one end and one of the cases swayed.

"Silly Willie Wash-er!" Sabina choked and started again, and all at once two packing-cases fell with a crash and Willie came rushing towards them, waving his arms and shouting the angry abuse which used to delight the children who baited him.

For the first time Brock let go Sabina's hand, and in a moment had pinioned the boy in a strong relentless grip.

"Quick, run back!" he said. "Tell the men outside to be ready so he doesn't give us the slip when we get him out. Hurry! This place won't be safe much longer."

She did not question his ability to bring Willie out single-handed, but did as she was bid. She found anxious faces waiting for her and said quickly:

"We've got him . . . don't be rough with him, will you? He did it for a purpose that was perfectly reasonable to him and he isn't really responsible."

"Laying the ghost, I reckon," the man called Bud said surprisingly.

"Yes; how did you know?"

"Everyone hereabouts knows young Willie Washer's mazed notions," he replied with rough kindliness. "Don't

187

be afeared for 'e, miss, I'll take 'n 'ome o' me. The missus has a wonderful way with sick animals and children."

But Willie, when he stood in safety on the grass below the first terrace, gave no more trouble. He gazed up at the burning house with child-like wonder and delight, and when Bud told him that it was time to go home, the boy went with him without protest.

The other men went back to the front of the house, where the fire brigade had at last arrived and were working too late on a hopeless task.

"Do you want to stay and watch?" asked Brock, his eyes resting on her with curious intensity.

"No," she said, and without conscious directions began walking from one sloping terrace to another towards the broken door in the wall. She leaned against it, pulling off her cap, and the wind whipped the hair back from her tired face.

"What will become of Willie?" she asked sadly. "Will he go to prison?"

"No," Brock answered with gentleness. "To a home, I expect; but that would really be best for him, you know. He's a lonely creature."

"Yes. I always felt a fellow feeling for him. He was trying to help you in his muddled, crazy fashion, you know."

"Yes, I know, and perhaps he has."

She looked up at him unhappily. The burning house cast a ruddy glow on his face, accentuating the sharp, forbidding lines of his features; the dominant nose and the hard, unyielding mouth. Sabina sighed.

"Yes, perhaps he has. You don't have to marry me now," she said.

He took her by the shoulders and gave her a sharp shake.

"My darling child! Was there ever any woman with such a poor opinion of herself as you?" he exclaimed, and oddly enough he was laughing. "I believe you're still convinced that the elderly M. Bergerac was only after Penruthan!"

"Well, you were, weren't you?" she said. "You were here on holiday to look it over, just like me, missing

188

poor Tante by a day. You had made plans for it."

"No," he said a little roughly. "I knew all along the house wasn't worth the money it would cost to put it to rights. Mine was a sentimental pilgrimage, that's all."

The shouts of the men in the distance came faintly through the roar of wind and flame. Every so often a piece of masonry fell with a muffled crash, and even here in the shelter of the high wall, smuts settled on Sabina's hair.

"Then why—" she began, her wide-set eyes suddenly enormous, but he pulled her abruptly into his arms.

"If you were going to ask anything so idiotic as why did I want to marry you, then my answer is why do you think?" he said. "Sabina, my poor shorn lamb, Bunny says that women should be told the things men imagine they must know for themselves. I've been remiss in taking what you had to give me without explaining in so many words that I was a man with as much to give in return. Did you really not know I had fallen in love with you?"

"No . . . no, I didn't . . ." she said, and at the humorous but somehow anxious tenderness in his face, the tears came. She put up her hands to draw his head down to hers, and although she could not speak, he felt her tears wet and warm on his cheek.

"You will still," he said to give her time, "have a husband with a physical infirmity, I'm afraid, though not, as you had imagined, a weak digestion. As to the elderly *roué* well—there's no smoke without a fire—which is, perhaps, something of a cliché with one already blazing behind us, but—I've had my *affaires* since my climbing days were over. Shall you mind?"

She raised her face then, and he traced the charming crescents of her lips and eyelids with a possessive finger.

"No, I shan't mind," she said, "any more than I mind the detruction of Penruthan, for now we are two and two."

"Two and two?"

"Yes. *One is One and all alone and ever more shall be so.* . . . That used to frighten me, you know. It's funny, but coming here in the train, I couldn't get those couplets out of my mind."

"Is this another of your rhymes?"

189

"Yes," she said. "I can't remember all of it. Shall I recite you what I know?"

"Yes, please," he replied gravely, because he could see that she was quite exhausted.

Thy stood there in the flickering light while she repeated those strange couplets for him, making them sound like a spell.

> Seven for the Seven who dwell in Heaven
> Six for the Six Proud Walkers.
> Five for the Flamboys under the boat,
> Four—

"I can't remember four."

"Never mind, we must go home. Bunny will be getting anxious, and you've got a smut on your nose."

She rubbed her nose absently with the back of her hand, smudging the smut to a sooty smear.

"Need we go back by the house? I don't want to see your old home blackened and charred."

"There's a path outside the wall, running back to the road," he said. "Didn't you find it?"

"No."

"We must have made it when I was a boy and the village children used to come up and play and weren't allowed inside. Come, I'll show you."

"You too?" she said softly, and her heart lifted as she took the hand he held out to her. He was not so different, she thought, stepping through the broken door to meet the fury of the wind; beneath that protective armour he was solitary and vulnerable as herself . . .

The broken door swung to behind them for the last time, and they walked in mutual silence down the rough dark path to the road.

JOY ROMANCE LOVE

Harlequin Omnibus

THREE love stories in ONE beautiful volume

The joys of being in love ...
the wonder of romance ...
the happiness that true love brings ...

Now yours in the HARLEQUIN OMNIBUS
edition every month wherever
paperbacks are sold.

And there's still *more* love in

Harlequin Presents...

Yes!

Six more spellbinding
romantic stories every month
by your favorite authors.
Elegant and sophisticated tales of
love and love's conflicts.

Let your imagination be swept away to
exotic places in search of adventure,
intrigue and romance. Get to
know the warm, true-to-life
characters. Share the special
kind of miracle that
love can be.

Don't miss out. Buy now and discover
the world of HARLEQUIN PRESENTS...